"From, "The Musty Old Magical Curiosity Shop, especiall...

THE MUS ___ED
MAGICAL CURIOSITY SHOP

Dianne Carol Sudron

ARTHUR H. STOCKWELL LTD
Torrs Park   Ilfracombe   Devon
Established 1898
www.ahstockwell.co.uk

British Library Cataloguing-in-Publication Data.
A catalogue record for this book is available
from the British Library.

ISBN 978-0-7223-4047-9
Printed in Great Britain by
Arthur H. Stockwell Ltd
Torrs Park   Ilfracombe
Devon

Contents

Milly Paris, the Silly Clock
That Couldn't Tell the Time

Milly Paris was hanging on the kitchen wall sobbing her heart out – big wailing sobs. "I feel so silly and stupid," she lamented.

"Dry your eyes, silly," cried Omega Horizon "or someone will surely hear you!"

Milly Paris was a very special kitchen wall clock, handmade in France with an antique, creamy, nicely painted face and large French numbers; but back in 'tickety-tock' classes in France she hadn't properly learnt to tell the time, or anything like it. She had only learnt to sing and socialise, and she talked in fluent English, French, and German. She was elegant and eloquent.

She had manners and sophistication, understood etiquette and was very humorous and silly. She was happy, funny and hilarious to be with, and she could be scandalous! However, she hadn't attended any of the 'tickety-tock' classes and hadn't learnt any time-telling skills. She either guessed it, or she asked the wristwatch Omega Horizon. Sometimes she even asked Charles Brown, a wristwatch purchased from Swiss Cottage in London – if he was lying on the kitchen top doing nothing! Very occasionally she asked the cat or the owl, but things had to be pretty bad before she would ask the silly fat cat.

Milly lived in a large Victorian house in Bayswater with Dr and Mrs Laugherty and their two children, Daisy and Oliver, their fat cat, Mog Og, and their butler, Miles Butterworth. They had all lived in France, in the city of Paris, but when they returned to London they moved into a large rambling house in a very prestigious area of Bayswater.

They loved France and the hot French weather. They had bought a French chateau, but it had needed a lot of renovation and they decided to keep it for a holiday place when renovations were completed.

Dr Patrick Laugherty's wife, Penelope (or Penny, as she liked to be called), was a journalist for a paranormal magazine called *Paranormal Investigations*.

Patrick was a handsome man with dark, wavy-brown, thick hair. He was stockily built and of medium height with green eyes. Penelope said he looked like an Irish potato farmer, and indeed his forefathers had come over from Ireland.

Patrick and Penelope liked to grow their own vegetables, and they had a vine that was growing in their greenhouse. It was very productive, and Miles helped to make about thirty bottles of wine from the grapes.

Penelope was of slim build. She had long fair hair, which she tinted blonde. She had soulful brown eyes. Patrick said she could have been a dancer at the Moulin Rouge, as she was very fit and athletic and loved to dance. She also enjoyed holding themed dinner parties, and she loved her job as a journalist.

Of course, she was always writing articles about the strange and unusual, but she didn't realise that the strangest and most unusual things went on in her own home.

She was so busy looking for the strange and unusual elsewhere that she never thought to look within her own family.

Penelope also enjoyed 1930s and 1940s wartime-themed events. Some people went to these events dressed in military uniforms and others wore more elegant, glamorous clothes in the styles of the 1930s and 1940s. Penelope and Patrick usually chose to wear elegant and glamorous clothes, but some of their friends chose military uniforms.

They had recently been to such an event on Patrick's thirty-fifth birthday. It had been held at Portmadog in Wales, and it had been such great fun. Some of the people looked as if they had come straight from the 1930s and 1940s – as if they had been beamed through a portal in time.

Dr Laugherty loved to be very punctual; he hated to be late. He was almost regimental about it. This approach to being on time was because of his job: he didn't want to keep his patients waiting.

Penelope had a high-pressure job, working to deadlines, and her work could take her away for weekends. Sometimes she had to go to Paris, in which case punctuality had to be the order of the day. If possible, she would catch a flight and be back the same day, as she hated to be away from home.

Both of their children, Daisy and Oliver, had a chauffeur to take them to school. The chauffeur was also the butler, Miles Butterworth, and he too was on time for everything – an impeccable example of punctuality. He had to be the support for the whole family. He owned an excellent wristwatch, Elijah Dual Movement, and he had a digital watch from Japan that was aptly named Zanuzy Zeon. Zanuzy could locate geographical landmarks like a compass. Miles also owned an alarm clock that actually spoke. He was named Preston Snooze and he had been made in South Carolina in the USA. He spoke with a Southern drawl. He was a military clock.

"Hi, buddy. This is the voice of Preston Snooze. I do declare that you, my buddy, must wake up and get your clothes on at once. There's no time like the morning – so good morning, buddy. I'm here for you if you're here for me. Right, let's wash and go-go-go-go-go!"

It was raining hard outside and grey clouds were hanging overhead. Milly thought that it was seven o'clock because the silly fat cat always strolled into the kitchen at that time.

"I guess it's seven o'clock," she whispered to Mog Og, the silly fat cat.

He replied as he straightened his crumpled whiskers after a good night's sleep, "You could say that, Milly. I guess it is." Then he wrinkled his forehead as he thought, and he asked, "What did you do in Paris, Milly? What did you learn, cos you seem to guess the time so much? Anyway, Milly, I'm gonna have to go through the cat flap into the pouring rain to do a whoopsie. Catch ya later, babe."

Max Life

Dr Patrick Laugherty had an alarm clock named Max Life. He had been made in Chicago and he woke Patrick up by singing in a booming voice. He sang, "It's time to rise and shine to a beautiful morning. It's time to wake up and shake off the night before. It's time to have a cup of tea, coffee or freshly squeezed orange juice, buttered toast, marmalade, soft-boiled eggs, hard-boiled eggs, cornflakes or sausage, beans and eggs, sunny side up. It's time to rise and shine and open your sleepy eyes. Remember your dreams – they can be so real even though they're so silly. You dreamt you put your pyjamas in the fridge and you tried to wear banana skins as a pair of shoes and slipped over. That was a really funny dream!" boomed the voice of Max Life. Max also gave dieting advice and a thermometer reading if Patrick ever got a sore throat, and he also took blood pressure and cholesterol readings.

Max Life always cheered Patrick up – and he was exactly the cheerful medicine he needed before he headed to his doctor's surgery to see his patients for that day.

As he scribbled out his prescriptions he would hum or sing, "Large boiled eggs, buttered toast and marmalade, gingerbread, cookies and large brown pears," and it certainly took the patients' minds off their problems.

He sometimes offered advice from Max Life instead of prescribing tablets; and sometimes the patients went out humming as they looked at their prescriptions and saw the words 'Raspberry juice, pineapple juice, ginger juice, orange juice and large brown pears, walnuts, coconuts and mangoes'. The patients went out laughing to themselves, definitely feeling 100 per cent better.

Dr Laugherty could write at speed, like all doctors can, and the lists were sometimes very long. He didn't always give out painkilling tablets, but he believed that happiness, laughter and healthy foods are often the best remedies for illnesses. He was a clever man.

Zimex Jones

All of the Laugherty family had wristwatches, and they were all very different. They all had different personalities, and different talents, just like people. They all got their watches in different ways — some of them were very strange.

One of the strangest watches was Daisy's watch. She got a watch when she was thirteen years old, and he was named Zimex Jones. He was just like something out of *Indiana Jones and the Temple of Doom*. Zimex Jones was in fact from another universe — in fact a parallel world in the fifth dimension. He originally belonged to a thirteen-year-old girl in that parallel world. She was also called Daisy — well, sort of: it was actually spelt DayZ. This DayZ from the parallel world had lost her wristwatch (never to be found again) and it had appeared on the Laugherty's sofa one night.

Mrs Laugherty thought that Patrick had put it there as a present for Daisy's thirteenth birthday, which happened to be the next day, so Penelope had gone and immediately wrapped it up in pink fancy paper with a gift tag saying, 'Surprise birthday pressie from Mum & Dad, Oliver & Mog Og. Lots of love and kisses on your 13th birthday'. Penelope put it in a pink-and-purple fancy bag. To this day, Penelope thinks Patrick bought it and Patrick thinks Penelope bought it.

Miles had a sense of humour. Chatting over tea one day

(using a real Ming dynasty china cup and saucer), he asked Mog Og if he'd bought it! It was as if Miles knew that nobody had bought it.

So that's how Zimex Jones became the wristwatch of Daisy Laugherty. One day in the future, maybe the two Daisys will swap places – maybe only for a day. That would be great fun. Daisy never dreamt something like that could happen, and in the parallel world DayZ was still perplexed and searching for her wristwatch.

Zimex Jones could 'time slip', and time-travelling modes were on his clock-face menu. How this worked for Daisy was that when she was late for school she had to keep looking at the watch. Daisy would be thirty minutes early for school if she looked at her watch thirty times, so she soon worked out that the watch slowed down time, and she had a gut instinct – just as many animals have – that the watch was from a parallel world. She also discovered that the watch when viewed through a mirror didn't look like a mirror image. Nothing was in reverse as it should have been.

She had been reading a book about Einstein and his theory of relativity, and another book on time travel which hadn't quite answered all of her questions, so she was still searching for answers and clues.

Daisy's favourite aunt was called Madeleine, and she was French. Madeleine had bought a doll from the Musty Old Magical Curiosity Shop when the musty old shop had materialised in Petticoat Lane during the Second World War. Madeleine had the doll as a young girl, and the doll had been given to Daisy for her sixth birthday. Madeleine had told Daisy about the musty old shop. The doll was named Anabella. She was a very pretty doll. She was dressed in a green velvet jacket with gold buttons and a cream floral-patterned pinafore over the top of a green velvet dress. She also had 1860s-style boots and a French beret with a cream ostrich feather. Anabella was a talking doll, and she sometimes gave secrets away — especially at midnight when the moon was full.

Well, one day Anabella whispered to Daisy that the wristwatch came from DayZ, who existed in a parallel world, and that the watch had actually fallen down a sofa (or a 'squashy-squishy recliner' as they were called in that world).

Camping in the Brecon Beacons

Sometimes the family spent a weekend camping, which was a bit of a headache for Miles as he had to organise everything. All the family loved the countryside. They thought being out in nature, sleeping under the stars, was the best medicine. Dr Laugherty had a very stressful job, and the best remedy for him was getting closer to nature, though he still liked to have the butler and the best food whilst they were camping.

Miles sometimes stayed up late into the night when they were camping. He waited until the last embers of the campfire had died down, and then he sometimes took out the telescope to look at the stars. The children also loved learning about the constellations, such as the Great Bear, the Giraffe, the Eagle, the Dolphin, the Hunting Dogs and all the zodiac constellations. They enjoyed going camping, and they enjoyed singing round the campfire and telling stories. Sometimes they were ghost stories, but if the ghost stories were too scary, Miles would be asked to stay up all night to ward off any ghosts.

Even Mog Og went on the camping trips, and even he would get very scared by the ghost stories. When he went to sleep he had nightmares.

Patrick and Penelope didn't like some of the really scary ghost stories Miles told.

Sometimes they had a glass of sherry before bedtime, served on a silver tray by Miles, who'd wear his butler suit even when camping. He had very little time to relax, but he enjoyed it that way. He got up early and went to bed later than everyone else, but he did enjoy camping under the stars. He felt most refreshed by it.

Sometimes when they went camping, strange and scary things happened. When camping, you can get creepy crickets making noises all night long and other strange noises; you get ants in your tent and large spiders coming in. You have to be prepared – well prepared – but it's great fun.

Sometimes the wristwatches helped out if anything was creeping about.

Oliver had received his wristwatch for his tenth birthday. The watch was named Julian Quartz and lit up in the dark. It lit up neon blue, argon green, jasper red, vivid violet, ochre yellow and oasis orange. This was an especially good watch, and it came in very handy when the family went camping – which they often did at weekends.

One particular weekend they went to the Brecon Beacons in Wales. Oliver was in his tent at the foot of the Brecon Beacons. He had heard that some of the locals had seen strange lights in the sky and heard an almighty crash. It could have been thunder or an earth tremor – or aliens landing.

As he lay in the tent the thought of this was making his heart pound. It was pitch-black in the tent – panther black – blacker than Welsh coal dust. The slightest noise set his hair on end and his teeth chattering. Suddenly he heard a strange bleating noise and something huge brushed against the tent. All at once Julian Quartz lit up and the whole tent was bathed in an eerie neon-blue light – and the creature outside the tent disappeared. Oliver was glad of the light from the watch, and he was glad that whatever it was had disappeared!

The watch also emitted a laser beam. It could stun strangers and hypnotise them, but it could only be used in an emergency. So far Oliver had never had to use it, but he knew that when the laser beam came into action a voice said, "This is an emergency – an emergency." He could switch the voice off if he wanted to, so as not to scare everyone.

On this particular night in the Brecon Beacons it was only a stray sheep outside the tent. The watch somehow knew this and reassured Oliver.

"It was a stray sheep. It was three years old. It was a pet sheep from Mr Ewan Evans' farm. It was called Woolley."

Woolley was sleepwalking, bumping into tents and scaring everyone inside.

"Thank goodness for that!" declared Oliver. "I thought it was an alien from outer space."

None of the other family members woke up. Daisy didn't wake up; nor did Penelope or Patrick; nor did Miles. Mog Og was in a tent of his own, and he didn't wake up either. He was on a well-earned vacation.

Only Oliver woke up.

They all had a laugh next morning over breakfast. They all realised something must have gone bump in the night as Oliver's hair was stuck up on end. He had to comb it ten times before it finally flattened into place. In fact, he had to put a bit of hair gel on it to flatten it. His hair was dark brown like Patrick's hair, and it was thick and curly.

Unfortunately the hair gel attracted flies, wasps and bees, as he soon found out. All day long Miles had to help to keep the flies, wasps and bees at bay, and sometimes Oliver ended up running like a wild thing to get away from them. Daisy found this funny. She laughed so much! Eventually Oliver had to take a shower and wash his hair. He had so many flies and midges stuck to it.

That was a hilarious camping holiday in Wales – at least, Daisy thought so. Oliver was glad Julian Quartz had come to his rescue, so he was quite happy.

Miles had had a good view of the night sky, and Penelope and Patrick had had a well-earned vacation out in the country air.

George Midnight and Jasmine Feathersprings

One autumn day Milly was feeling lonely, and she was feeling a bit under the weather. It was windy outside and the leaves were falling off the big oak tree. The summer was over. It felt like the fun had suddenly gone. What Milly wanted was some fun company.

"I wouldn't mind having some more clock friends, Omega," piped up Milly.

"Well, you have me, Milly, to talk to, don't forget."

"Well, you're not always around. You're a wristwatch, Omega, and you spend a lot of time on Mrs Laugherty's wrist gallivanting about while I'm stuck on this wall!"

That was true, but Omega Horizon did spend quite a lot of time sitting on the kitchen table or on the kitchen worktop or on a shelf of the Welsh dresser.

Omega liked to listen into conversations, and she had a photographic memory. Basically she recorded conversations, and Mrs Laugherty often left the wristwatch sitting in the kitchen to record any conversation without anyone knowing they were being recorded. Mrs Laugherty also wore the wristwatch a lot, which was very useful where she worked.

"Well," said Milly, "Mrs Laugherty said she wanted to buy a grandfather clock for the hall and a cuckoo clock for the dining room and possibly a clock for the drawing room and one for the living room, but do you think she ever will?" Milly sighed forlornly.

"Of course she will, if she can find them in one of those antique shops that she sometimes goes into."

"Well," said Milly excitedly, "I think you could help with this, Omega. When you're on Mrs Laugherty's wrist you could keep your eyes peeled; and if you see something – or you see an antique shop – give her a nudge. If you come across a grandfather clock – even if he's a bit eccentric or mad – or an old cuckoo clock that works, of course I would be very happy."

"I will see what I can do, Milly. I will keep my eyes open and try to get Mrs Laugherty in a dusty old antique shop."

"Oh, you're so kind, Omega," cried Milly.

A few weeks later Penelope Laugherty was walking along the High Street in Bayswater and she happened to come across a shop she hadn't seen before – at least, not that she could recall. It was the Musty Old Magical Curiosity Shop.

She immediately felt drawn to it. It looked fascinating, so she went in and browsed round. Cobwebs and dust hung in the corners of the shop, and the old shopkeeper who owned it looked very old indeed. He had a long beard, a bespectacled face and a dusty old pinstriped suit.

Suddenly the old shopkeeper asked, "Are you by any chance interested in a grandfather clock and a cuckoo clock?"

They were in the far corner of the shop, almost hidden from view under a thick layer of cobwebs. Penelope asked if they worked.

"Of course they work. Why wouldn't they work? I think they would love to be purchased by you."

The old shopkeeper went over to the clocks and brushed off the cobwebs with a feather duster. Suddenly the clocks woke up as if they had been asleep. The grandfather clock sneezed.

"Yes," said Penelope. "I have a large Victorian house. It has a wide hallway, and high-heeled shoes make a clippety-clop sound on the black-and-white tiled floor. I think the grandfather clock would be perfect for the hallway, and I think the cuckoo clock would be splendid to have on the wall just next to the china cabinet in my dining room. I am looking for clocks that keep perfect time," said Penelope. She was thinking out loud.

"As perfect as time itself!" said the old shopkeeper. "Well, guess what? Look no further, my dear. A couple of minor adjustments and they will be working as if brand new."

Omega was listening to the conversation intently. She was so excited, and she couldn't wait to get home and tell Milly about the great find. However, Omega thought it was strange to find such perfect clocks in a shop so full of cobwebs. She began to wonder if they did actually work.

Penelope arrived home feeling very cheerful, and when Patrick got home from a busy day at the surgery she told him of the great find. She had wasted no time, and they had been delivered that day. The grandfather clock was stood in the hallway, looking proud as Punch. His name was George Midnight. The cuckoo clock was on the wall in the dining room. Her name was Jasmine Feathersprings and she was feeling over the moon. She had a little smile on her face.

Patrick rushed into the hallway to inspect George, and he was very impressed. Then he went into the dining room, where Jasmine was happily sitting on the wall. He went right up to her to inspect her, and he got a big surprise when the cuckoo clock started shouting.

"Cuckoo! Cuckoo! Cuckoo!"

The bird flew out in front of him, nearly hitting him in the face.

Mog Og was asleep on the mat, but he was rudely awoken. He wasn't so impressed by the noise – or the idea of a bird being in the house, rudely shouting and yelling. Mog Og didn't share the family's enthusiasm. He thought to himself that he would somehow get the cuckoo to stop squawking. But for the present he decided to pretend to be pleasant, friendly and courteous.

A Night Out

Omega Horizon excitedly told Milly all about the new clocks. At last Milly would have some new friends to help her tell the time when Omega was on Mrs Laugherty's wrist. Mog Og wasn't always around, as he sometimes stayed out all night, like most cats do now and then.

One night Mog Og went out through the cat flap. It was raining, and Mog Og decided that he'd have a little dance. He started to dance and sing 'I'm Singing in the Rain'. He spun round and round and jumped on the fence, where he continued to dance. Well, Mog Og got carried away, and the female ginger cat next door, Marmalade, came out to see what all the noise was about. She saw Mog Og dancing, and before long they were both dancing together, doing the cha-cha, the jitterbug and the waltz in quick succession. It was great fun. When the moon came out they were still dancing and singing.

Eventually Mog Og, feeling very romantic, escorted Marmalade home. He was so tired that he ended up staying at Marmalade's place, and he fell asleep on her fluffy rug, curled up next to her.

Next morning Mog Og had a bit of a shock when he woke up and saw Marmalade. He decided to sneak out of her house as fast as he could because he felt so embarrassed. He was sure he must have been drunk on the moonlight and the dancing.

He left Marmalade sleeping, and he sneaked out as fast as he could. He jumped over the fence and through his own cat flap and curled up on his own rug in front of his own fire.

Milly, sitting on the wall, saw the cat sneaking past. She knew Mog Og had been out all night.

A few minutes later Mog Og strolled into the kitchen as if he'd been in the house all night.

He said to Milly, "Oh, Milly, I feel as though I've been out all night on the tiles."

"Really, Mog Og?" said Milly. "You normally sleep like a log."

"Well, I'm just going to have a bit of a slurp of milk, and then I'm gonna go back to sleep and have a bit of a catnap."

Then Mog Og strolled back out of the kitchen.

'No change there, then!' thought Milly. 'I'll not see Mog Og for about ten hours now. I'll have to occupy myself.'

Then she realised she now had the grandfather clock and the cuckoo clock to talk to if she could muster up the courage to strike up a conversation.

Suddenly she felt very excited at the thought that she had more friends in the house that she could ask for help, instead of hoping that Mog Og would come into the kitchen for a slurp from his milk saucer. 'God!' she thought. 'That fat cat's so predictable. When he's at home he comes in for a drink every ten minutes.'

Suddenly Mog Og was strolling into the kitchen.

"Hi, Milly. How are you tocking and ticking?"

"I'm cool, Mog Og. You seem in a good mood – anything happened?"

"Well, to be honest, Milly," said Mog Og slowly, "I went out last night and I danced in the rain in the moonlight with Marmalade. We had a few kisses and cuddles. I think I'm in love. I think she's the one."

"I'm glad you're happy, Mog Og."

"I definitely am, Milly. I'm gonna go and have another catnap and just dream about her. Catch ya, later!" Mog Og swanned out of the kitchen, singing 'I'm As Cool As Custard and Hot As Mustard' and he curled up on his fluffy rug feeling like the cat that got the cream. In no time at all he was enjoying a groovy dream about his ginger lady-love, Marmalade.

Dr Rama Singh

The leaves were falling off the trees and there was a slight coolness in the morning air. Patrick thought they needed to have a party and invite their friends. It was also Penelope's birthday on 31 October, so they decided to have a 1920s-themed cocktail party to brighten up the dreary autumn.

"Penelope," said Patrick one morning, "what we'll do is to have a cocktail party with a 1920s-themed buffet, and we'll have all the 1920s paraphernalia. We could even hire a 1920s car. And, sweetie, I'm going to give you some money so you can buy yourself something from that antique shop you've been to. Those clocks have been just perfect, and there might be something else there you would like. I know you were over the moon with your bargain-hunting in that shop. You know, Penelope, I miss France and the warm French climate. I miss croissants for breakfast, and French wine, Notre-Dame and the Champs Elysées. We must find something amusing to do in the dreary autumn and winter in London."

Patrick loved the warm weather, and he always liked to have friends around the house in the dark winter months. Penelope didn't mind the autumn and winter. She wore long skirts and boots and jumpers, a fur hat, a thick coat and gloves. As long as you wear the right clothes you should feel OK. Possibly the real reason Patrick didn't look forward to the colder time of year was that he had more patients with colds and flu at the surgery, and some of these patients suffered the winter blues. In his surgery, just to make him feel as though it were summertime for ever, he had a large picture of the French lavender fields with deep azure skies. He also had an aquarium with tropical fish, potted palms, a large picture of a tropical scene with orange-tinted skies, blue sea, palm trees and tropical birds in flight. He had a walnut office desk and brown leather upholstered armchairs. Everything was so cosy and upbeat that sometimes the patients wanted to stay for ever, chatting away.

Patrick had trained in hypnotherapy. He certainly wasn't a conventional doctor. He believed in the power of herbs and lotions and potions, the power of prayer, the power of mind and the ability to bring out the magic in the mind. He believed in analysing dreams and trying to gain an understanding of them. His great ambition was to go to the Brazilian rainforest and study the plants there in order to find a cure for common illnesses. Above all, he hoped to find plants that can heal the mind. He also believed laughter was very healing, and he always managed to laugh and joke with his patients. He was very charming and amusing, with his wavy dark-brown hair and green twinkling eyes. His father was a doctor, so it was in his blood, so to speak. He was very popular. He had the Irish twinkle in his eye, and his grandparents were from County Cork in Ireland.

His grandparents had owned an apothecary business. They sold a face cream for wrinkles which contained lanolin mixed with wild honey and the herb comfrey. They had land and kept sheep. From the sheep's wool the family all had hand-knitted woollen jumpers, and even today Patrick loved wearing hand-knitted jumpers. He was also fond of bow ties. He was a bit of a trend setter, or maybe a fashion icon – a doctor with a taste and flair for fashion.

It was his intention that one day, when the chateau in France was renovated, he would have sheep, so he could have his jumpers hand-knitted using wool from his own flock.

He decided that all his sheep would have names. They would be classed as 'pet sheep' – they certainly wouldn't go to the slaughterhouse. He also wanted to have cows, whose dung could be used on campfires instead of logs. He had plenty of plans, all in his head. Hopefully, with a bit of luck and elbow grease, some of his ambitions would actually happen. He believed they would.

He believed getting out in nature was an ideal therapy for body, mind and soul, and that is why he went camping so much. He knew that the open air had a unique feel-good factor. It was good for the morale.

He thought that when the chateau was renovated he would have a vineyard. There was already a bit of a vineyard on the property, but it needed some work done on it. It was very tangled with weeds. He decided to have free-range chickens and maybe some goats to provide milk and cheese. He discussed his plans with his patients, and some of them offered to help out with the vineyard. No doubt they were eager to get a few glasses of French wine!

This shows exactly how friendly Patrick was.

Now, Patrick had a friend who was a Sikh. He wore a turban, which was always the same colour as his clothes. If he wore a green suit, he wore a green turban; and if he wore a white suit, he wore a white turban. His name was Dr Rama Singh and he spoke with an Indian accent as he was from New Delhi, in India. He was a research doctor. Patrick was fascinated by him because he always said strange things, and he had a watch that would suddenly chant strange words. It could also create rainbows in the sky when it was raining. It cheered his patients up to see a rainbow out of the surgery window.

One day Patrick asked him if there could be a pot of gold at the end of the rainbow.

Dr Singh said he was 100 per cent sure of it.

The Australian Clock

A few days before Penelope's birthday, on 31 October, Miles decided to buy her a birthday present.

Penelope loved Australia and she had an aunt and uncle that lived there. Their names were Sheila and Bruce. Penelope wanted to visit Australia. She regularly exchanged emails with Sheila and Bruce. Penelope had received a cuddly fluffy koala bear and fluffy kangaroos for birthday and Christmas presents for the children, and this inspired Miles to get something handmade in Australia for Penelope.

Miles had a few hours to spare, so he popped out of the house and walked along the Bayswater Road. He was going to the dry cleaner's to pick up his best velvet butler suit and bow tie. It had needed cleaning as gravy and cranberry sauce had been spilt on it at Christmas. Well, he was just about to go into the dry cleaner's, which was named Clean as a Whistle, when he suddenly saw the Musty Old Magical Curiosity Shop. It was next to a barber's shop named Hair Today, Gone Tomorrow. He thought he would pop into the curiosity shop to look for something suitable for Penelope's birthday.

He walked into the shop, and straight away a very unusual wooden clock came to his attention. It was shaped like the land mass of Australia, and it had a cute little koala-bear motif in the middle of it. On the back it said, 'Made in Queensland, Australia'. It looked fabulous.

"I really must have that," said Miles to the shopkeeper.
The shopkeeper looked very strange to Miles. He was wearing a pointed purple hat decorated with stars that twinkled like real stars. His eyes were piercing like X-rays. They went right through Miles's body and made him feel as though the man knew everything from A to Z.

In the shop window a tree grew out of the ground. The top branches poked out of a window in the roof, and in the tree an owl perched. It had huge eyes, which opened once in a while, and the owl was talking away to himself. Next to the owl, on a large purple cushion, sat a big white Persian cat with lime-green eyes – the colour of the leaves on the tree.

It said, "Oh, dearie me! Oh, dearie me! I'm a cat from the Musty Old Magical Curiosity Shop. I can't be sold because I'm so old, but not really ancient, and my name's Blug Blag Blig Blah. In other words, call me Lucky. If you say it three times, I will bring you luck all day."

Then the owl chipped in and said, "And my name's Hoot-Hoot. I will make you hoot all day with laughter. So come into the shop. We welcome thee. We have just about everything. We sell watches, fridges, bridges, ditches, cars, jars, pickled onions, walnuts, nougat, marzipan and frying pans. Erm, let me think – we also sell washing machines, dusters, spinning tops, groovers, movers, Hoovers, mobile phones, cherry scones, flapjacks, flip-flops, shirts, skirts, wedding rings, stars, televisions, Christmas hats, Christmas crackers, jokes, Mad Hatters, Christmas stockings, rocking chairs, looking glasses, oddments for the stairs, carpets, rugs, garden rakes, forks, trucks, rattlesnakes . . ."

It was an extremely long list – they seemed to have everything under the sun.

The shopkeeper wore a long purple robe, and Miles thought he looked like Merlin the Wizard. 'Perhaps he really is Merlin,' thought Miles.

29

The shopkeeper suddenly said, "You like it, then?"
Miles handed him the clock from Australia.

"Indeed I do," said Miles.

The shopkeeper's name was Mabble-babble-bobble-bibble-frabble-go-babble Merlin. It was such a long name that most people simply called him Merlin. Others called him Mabble Merlin or Mad Mab, because they thought he was absolutely crazy, 'nuts, whole hazelnuts' insane – completely bonkers, utterly barking mad, totally cuckoo or a buffoon. At any rate, he was definitely quirky, eccentric and odd. Moreover, the shop was always moving from place to place and everything in the shop was odd and magical.

Miles thought the shopkeeper had a very old face – older than time itself, some might say. He had a long beard, a moustache and tousled grey hair that sprung out of his head like that of a mad professor. He had mud-brown eyes, like owls' eyes, and sometimes he wore spectacles.

When a customer went into the shop he was never there, but suddenly he would pop up from behind the counter (or sometimes from out of thin air).

Sometimes inside the shop a little café bar would appear if the customer was feeling thirsty. It sold the tastiest, most mouth-watering food, including coffee, tea, milkshakes, muffins and scones. When a customer sat down, it wasn't unusual for him to stay there all day. Sometimes a cup of coffee lasted all day and long into the night. Sometimes a customer woke up, having fallen asleep, and the café bar would be totally different. At times it was like a futuristic space bar selling glasses of potions, including an orange substance that made your head spin right round the Milky Way and across the Crab Nebula.

Miles had been in the shop before, and on that occasion he had decided to sit and have a coffee. He therefore knew from experience how easy it would be to lose two days or more.

He thought, 'I'm just going to buy this Australian clock for Penelope's birthday.'

Then Mabble Merlin piped up: "Are you just buying the clock today, Miles?"

"Yes, just a birthday present for Penelope, you see."

"Well, Miles, the clock is named Polly Quazar. She is from Queensland in Australia."

"What type of wood is it made from?" Miles asked.

"Well," said Mabble Merlin, "it comes from a tree that only grows in the Lands of the Legends. They are mystical trees and they grow in fairy woods. Polly can speak, in her affectionate, loquacious way, and maybe she will tell you herself in her lovely, lively Australian accent. If you don't want her to speak, there is an on-off switch — if you ever find it! I don't suppose you ever will. You will find Polly very enigmatic. She is also telepathic and can read minds. You see, she was made in the Dreamtime using ancient Aboriginal skills, with jackals howling at the full moon. That can be wild and scary, let me tell you! The Aboriginals were playing their didgeridoos. Polly Quazar is special. For sure and definitely she is good enough for a special birthday present for a special person."

Anne Boleyn's Mirror

"Would you like a coffee or tea or a blueberry muffin, Miles?" asked Mabble Merlin.

"Well, I haven't really got time," said Miles, feeling a bit awkward.

"Oh, don't worry," said Mabble Merlin, we'll turn back the clock and you'll be back home before you went out this morning."

Miles looked at the shopkeeper with a quizzical look and wondered what on earth he could mean. But it sounded like a very good thing to be back before you went out, so the very next minute he heard himself asking for an exceedingly large latte and a most beautiful blueberry muffin that he suddenly saw on the cake stand. It was a Victorian cake stand and it seemed to go up to the ceiling. Miles lost count of how many tiers it had and how many different cakes, but there must have been almost every type he could think of.

No sooner had he asked for the muffin and latte than a large china cup and saucer were being brought out on a silver tray with the large, simply delicious-looking blueberry muffin. Actually it was a little bit of a secret, but the waitress was from King Henry VIII's court. She had been one of the King's many wives – he had six wives in all! When she came out holding the silver tray, dressed in regal costume, Miles kind of recognised her.

As Miles drank his coffee he looked into his coffee cup.

It was huge. He felt he was being hypnotised; he was definitely mystified. Reflected in the coffee cup he saw a scene from King Henry's court, and then he knew for certain that the waitress was one of Henry's wives. He wasn't sure which one, but he was sure it was a very strange thing indeed for any one of them to be a waitress in the Musty Old Magical Curiosity Shop in Bayswater on a fine Saturday morning. Miles was lost for words. He was dumbfounded. He couldn't quite add it all up and take it all in. Bayswater is a quite leafy area of London, and things very rarely happened there – at least, they had very rarely happened to Miles before he came to work for the Laugherty family. Since then many strange things had happened.

Miles sat pondering and drinking his coffee. The china cup was so large he felt he could almost take a swim in it, and yet it was so light. If he had known it was actually from the Ming dynasty, and was therefore hundreds of years old, he would certainly have been trembling a bit. As he drank the coffee, he was none the wiser that the cup came from the reign of one of the greatest Chinese emperors: Emperor Zao Ze Ming, famed for his chocolate army.

He took another bite of the blueberry muffin, savouring the taste. Then suddenly he nearly choked on the muffin as he realised which wife of Henry VIII's wives it was. It was none other than Anne Boleyn!

He nearly fell off the chair in disbelief. He turned to have another good look at her and noticed she was disappearing through a large old-fashioned standing mirror.

He jumped up off the chair and went to follow her, but he came face-to-face with his own reflection in the old-fashioned mirror. Then he noticed a label on the mirror. It said, 'Anne Boleyn's original dressing mirror'. He stared into the mirror, rooted to the spot as if hypnotised.

Suddenly there was a tap on his shoulder. Miles jumped out of his skin, but it was only the old shopkeeper, Mabble Merlin.

"Everything to your satisfaction, sir, with the blueberry muffin and coffee?" he asked.

"Y-y-y-yes," said Miles, stammering. "I – I was just appreciating this fabulous mirror. Erm, the label says it is Anne Boleyn's original mirror."

"Oh, yes," said Mabble Merlin matter-of-factly. "Yes, that's true. Anne Boleyn was very enamoured with the mirror. It made her look beautiful in her wedding dress, you see. She often just pops in to help out in the shop."

Miles was holding the coffee cup and, as he couldn't help but tremble, the coffee spilt. After all, he had just seen a ghost! But hey! she looked so fine, and she looked so alive. Good heavens, she'd just served him coffee and a blueberry muffin!

'Goodness me!' thought Miles.

He went back to the table to sit down. He was a bit shaken.

"So, she's – er – OK, then?" asked Miles tentatively.

"Oh, she's splendid. She's a great help in the shop when we're busy, and she loves London."

"She loves London!" repeated Miles. He was thunderstruck.

"Let's just say she loves, loves, loves London," said Mabble Merlin.

"She loves, loves, loves London!" repeated Miles.

For several minutes Miles just repeated everything Mabble Merlin said. He was lost for words.

But the coffee was marvellous. It made him feel so happy and joyful and gave him such a zest for life that suddenly it no longer bothered him that he couldn't figure out why Anne Boleyn had suddenly popped up, serving him coffee and a blueberry muffin. He felt that there were so many things to do, to see, to say – in fact, the shop was as full to the brim as anything ever could be.

He looked around the shop as he sat eating the rest of the very large blueberry muffin, and his head spun and his eyes began to blur. He focused his eyes and he suddenly noticed an exquisite pair of curtains made of rich burgundy silk brocade. They looked brand new. He also noticed a magnificent carpet.

"Where's that carpet from?" enquired Miles.

"That's from Persia, of course," said Mabble Merlin. "Have you heard of magic flying carpets, Miles?" enquired Mabble Merlin. "Well, that carpet is the original flying carpet from Aladdin's cave. The Genie of the Lamp often pops in with something to donate, and in return I have given a few things to the genie. The silk brocade curtains come from China – from the Ming dynasty. They are made from the silk of 1,000 million silkworms – handwoven – and they hold the million secrets of the Chinese sages of old."

The New Haircut

Suddenly Miles realised he'd been in the shop for at least three hours.

"Oh, my word! I must go. I must dash," declared Miles. "I didn't intend to stay for three hours."

Mabble Merlin declared, "When you walk out of here, only thirty minutes will have gone by."

It was perfectly true: Miles walked out into the brilliant sunshine, under a powder-blue sky and the swaying trees along the Bayswater Road, and only half an hour had gone by. Mabble Merlin had delicately wrapped up the quaint Australian clock in pink paper, with a ribbon tied in a bow, and popped it into a pink-and-purple-striped fancy carrier bag.

Polly Quazar was tickled pink and sky blue to be joining a new family in England – Bayswater of all places. She hoped to be making brand-new friends very soon. She knew (with her telepathic powers) that she would be living with a very interesting family in a grand Victorian town house in Bayswater, overlooking an oak-tree-lined street. Her dream had come true.

Miles breathed in the London air, which tasted sweeter than ever – just like nectar from a honeybee.

He dashed into the dry cleaner's to collect his cleaned butler's outfit – his bow tie, waistcoat, top hat and tails and black leather pointy-toed shoes.

On the door of Hair Today, Gone Tomorrow was a sign that read, 'Quiffs and Coiffed – special offers'. So Miles decided to pop into the barbershop to get his head quiffed and coifed and slicked into a 1920s-style slick hairdo. His moustache was teased and tweaked upwards until it almost looked part of a barbershop quartet.

Miles loved to sing, and he could play the drums, the piano, the violin, the mandolin, the double bass, the trumpet, the clarinet, the trombone, the bodhrán and the harpsichord. He also wrote music, and one day he hoped one of his classical compositions would be performed by a full orchestra. Though he loved his job as a butler, ever since Dr Laugherty had saved his life, he had an ambition to achieve.

Miles, believe it or not, used to ride a motorbike, and one wet Sunday afternoon he was going a little fast and he spun out of control. He went headlong into a lake. He was knocked out completely, but luckily Dr Laugherty and Penelope just happened to be having a romantic Sunday stroll by the lake that day. They saw a strange man on a motorbike go head first into the lake and disappear. Luckily Dr Laugherty was a scuba-diver, and he had learnt to swim while holding his breath underwater. He dived into the cold lake and fished poor Miles out. Poor old Miles survived with minor bumps, cuts and bruises and a bit of amnesia. Dr Laugherty offered him a job.

At that time the Laugherty's were moving to France, and Miles wanted to taste another cultural atmosphere and to learn to speak French and cook French cuisine. The family took off for Paris, and they lived there for three years. That was how Miles got the job: just by a chance meeting, albeit whilst he was drowning in the lake.

When he wasn't doing his butler duties, Miles sometimes sang for the family. His friends often came to the house, and they brought their instruments. They played the mandolin, the accordion, the violin, the glockenspiel, the piano and the drums – and they played them very well indeed!

London Melody

A few days after Miles had gone into the Musty Old Magical Curiosity Shop, it was Patrick's turn to go into the shop to buy a birthday present for Penelope.

Patrick was sitting in the surgery when in walked his good friend Dr Singh.

"I've come to take your blood pressure," he said as he walked in.

Patrick started laughing. "I need it," he said. "What a stressful day! Nearly every patient is feeling depressed and I can't think what to say. I had a call that one of my patients had gone all the way to Beachy Head to throw himself off the cliff – and what happened? Amazingly some geese flying by swooped down and plucked him out of the water, so he is OK."

"Wow!" said Dr Singh. "That's amazing! Who would have thought geese would do that!"

"Well, that's what witnesses said it was. I think it was an angel of the Lord, don't you? Anyway, Dr Singh, it's my Penelope's birthday. How do you fancy going up the Bayswater Road and helping to buy a pressie? We'll have a drink afterwards in the Lion the Witch and the Unicorn."

"OK," said Dr Singh.

He and Patrick went to the Bayswater area. They were walking along when suddenly Patrick saw the Musty Old Magical Curiosity Shop. It had sprung up again out of nowhere.

"I've never seen this shop before," said Dr Singh. "Is it for real?"

Patrick laughed and said, "It looks real enough, but I suspect it's from a parallel universe."

They both laughed their heads off.

They went in, and immediately Patrick noticed, at the same time as Dr Singh noticed it, a very large picture of London. It showed the Houses of Parliament and Big Ben and several London buses. The clock on Big Ben, seemed real.

"This will be great for a present for Penelope – a nice scene of London. It's so eye-catching."

"It certainly is!" said Dr Singh.

Mabble Merlin came over to them. This time he was wearing a pinstriped suit and bowler hat, just like a London gent. His hair was short, and he had no long beard or moustache, but he had the same mud-brown eyes like an owl's eyes. When Dr Singh saw him he started to laugh and couldn't stop. He didn't know what he was laughing at, but it all seemed so funny.

Mabble Merlin suddenly said, "The possibilities are endless."

"What?" said Patrick.

"I see you're admiring the picture of London," said Mabble Merlin. "Well, it's called London Melody, and the scene changes to show different scenes of London, including scenes of days gone by. As I was saying, the possibilities are endless. It's the motto of London Melody."

"Oh, I see," said Patrick.

Dr Singh was still laughing and trying not to, but Patrick remained poker-faced and took it all in his stride.

"I love the picture and the fact the scene changes – but what about the clock? Does it disappear?"

Dr Singh laughed again, but he tried to cough to disguise the laughter.

"Well," said Mabble Merlin, "you won't believe it but there is always a clock on the picture when the scene changes. The clock may be on a church, or it may be on St Paul's Cathedral, or you may see a tavern with a clock on it, or Big Ben may remain on the scene, or a shop may appear with a clock in the shop window – do you get my meaning?"

Dr Singh was still laughing. He wanted to get out of the shop as it felt so rude to be laughing when Patrick was trying to find out about the picture. Dr Singh got out his handkerchief and pretended he had a bit of a cold, but everything Mabble Merlin said made him laugh. Then suddenly Dr Singh saw the owl in the tree in the window of the shop.

The owl said, "You won't find empty spaces."

"What?" said Patrick.

"You won't find empty spaces on the picture, of course."

Patrick wondered if it was some sort of riddle, but Dr Singh just thought that it was a hilarious random thought. It didn't make sense, but neither did owls that spoke. Dr Singh wanted to hurry up and get out of the shop and go and get a drink – maybe a brandy would calm him down.

"I want to take the picture," said Patrick to Mabble Merlin.

"We'll have it delivered for you," said the shopkeeper. "You don't want to carry such a large picture through London – especially if you're going for a drink and a bit of something to eat."

"OK," said Patrick.

Dr Singh and Patrick walked out of the shop, and Dr Singh's fit of the giggles was gone – just like that!

They sat in the pub, and both had a Jack Daniels with a touch of soda. Patrick ordered lemon sole with organic vegetables, and Dr Singh ordered prawn curry, rice and poppadoms. They both pondered over London Melody and its motto, 'The possibilities are endless.' They both took a drink of whisky and looked at each other and burst out laughing.

Patrick said, "You must come to Penelope's birthday party. We're having a cocktail party on 31 October. It's themed: a 1920s cocktail party."

"Sounds like a great party!" said Dr Singh. "I wouldn't miss it for the world."

They came out of the pub and said their goodbyes.

The Midnight Prowl

Back home, Mog Og was getting ready for his midnight prowl. He always met a few male cats and a few lady cats at the same place every night. They met at the zebra crossing. Mog Og stood at the side of the crossing and waited till his mates came out to play. He was always on time, but the others were often late. One of his best mates was a big, fat, blacker-than-midnight cat called Barney – in fact, you couldn't see him in the dark.

While Mog Og stood at the crossing a few motorists went past and shouted horrible things at him.

"You scruffy, smelly moggy! Get out of here!"

Mog Og shouted back, "You stupid shirt-and-tie! Get out of my fur!"

Mog Og always had an answer – he was a wordsmith and knew what to say.

Well, Barney hadn't turned up. He was late again. And Marmalade hadn't turned up either, and neither had Mog Og's other mates, such as Popcorn, Marzipan, Cat Majick, Galaxy and Fudge. Mog Og sat twiddling his thumbs – or should I say *paws* – and pondering the universe.

Suddenly a bucketful of water landed squarely on his head. Someone from a bedroom window had chucked out some water. Actually they had a blocked sink and didn't know Mog Og was underneath the window.

At that moment Marmalade turned up, and Mog Og didn't know what to do. He was drenched to the skin.

Marmalade started laughing.

"Oh, dearie me! What's happened to you?"

"I got caught in a downpour, my darling! The shirt-and-tie upstairs chucked water on me. Let's have a good old sing-song and see if he likes it; or maybe I'll climb up the drainpipe, peep in his bedroom window and freak him out."

Marmalade laughed so much. She thought it was a great idea to climb up the drainpipe on to the window ledge and freak out the 'shirts-and-ties'.

Suddenly all their other friends turned up – even lazy Barney turned up.

"Hey, where've you been, Barney?"

"Sleeping, Mog Og. I've been busy sleeping, counting sheep."

"You must have counted a lot of sheep, then," said Mog Og.

"I am a cat, you know," said Barney, raising an eyebrow.

"Oh, I thought you were a mole or a vole," said Mog Og. "I think you should get yourself out here with us when it's midnight, instead of sleeping all the time. You're getting as fat as a cat in a hat."

"What's one of those, Mog Og?" said Barney.

"I've no idea, but I thought I'd say it. Anyway, the gossip is, I hear, that Marzipan fancies you a bit. Lucky you, eh, Barney?"

"She's a very sweet kitty-cat, so don't upset her or ignore her. Be very charming to her and you'll win her heart. Lucky you, Barney!"

"And am I going to meet any lovely young ladies of the night?" asked Popcorn.

"Well, I'll introduce you to Lady Treacle. I'm sure she'll be impressed. I'll also introduce you to her friends Coconut and Cleopatra."

That was how Mog Og and his cat friends spent their evening: gossiping and trying to meet new lady-cat friends.

The very next night Mog Og said to his cat friends, "Meet me beside the zebra crossing at midnight. Be there or be square."

Mog Og arrived briskly on time with a dab of eau de cologne. He was ready for the midnight mischief.

Mog Og waited at the zebra crossing, and not long after midnight Barney showed up. Mog Og was glad he didn't have to sit any longer on a bin lid twiddling his thumbs, pondering the mysteries of the universe and thinking up rhymes.

"Hey, I'm glad you showed up, Barney. Marzipan and Popcorn are not here yet."

"I think Marzipan will be late. She'll be washing her fur

and manicuring her nails. You know very well she's a glamour puss."

Barney and Mog Og walked on together along the same route they travelled every night. Every now and then they looked at the stars and tried to identify the Plough or the Pole Star. Suddenly Popcorn turned up with his friends Fudge and Cat Majick. Even Marzipan, looking glamorous, turned up.

"Hey, Mog Og," said Popcorn, "are you going to introduce me to Lady Treacle and Cleopatra and Coconut? I'm in the mood for lurv!"

"Well," said Mog Og, "they all live in a posh area of Hyde Park, and it's a bit of a journey down the cobblestones just past Kensington. It will be difficult to get them out on a chilly night like this. We'll have to sing or I'll have to sing as they all know my voice."

"Well," said Popcorn, "I will be over the moon if you can tempt them out, because they sound like the cutest girl cats I'll ever have the good fortune to meet. It's so worth trying to tempt them out with your best singing. Me and Barney will accompany you."

"Come on, then," said Mog Og. "Let's go and introduce you to the girls."

Mog Og and Barney and Popcorn stood under the street lamps on the tree-lined avenue where Lady Treacle and Cleopatra and Coconut lived. Mog Og started to sing a love song in his best voice, and Popcorn and Barney sang the chorus.

Lady Treacle was the first to hear them singing. She recognised Mog Og immediately, and she ran out to meet her old friend.

As soon as she noticed Barney, it was love at first sight. She loved his black fur. Barney was rather shy, but he and Lady Treacle struck up a friendship while Popcorn waited patiently for the other girls to come out. Mog Og continued to sing.

At last Cleopatra and Coconut strolled along the avenue to meet the boys. Popcorn fell in love with Cleopatra. Her black satin fur and long eyelashes caught his eye; Mog Og preferred the milky satin fur of Coconut, who walked so elegantly. Coconut looked at Mog Og and smiled a very sweet smile.

"I'm so glad you've managed to get out, my dear," said Mog Og.

"I heard you singing," said Coconut. "I must admit that love song was beautiful."

When Coconut spoke her voice was like velvet satin. Mog Og was lost for words. He was a wordsmith – he could make up songs and poetry – but he was lost for words when Coconut spoke.

Suddenly Lady Treacle suggested they all go to her house and chill out on the back porch. Lady Treacle had a tree house in the garden, and she thought it was an ideal pad for her and Barney. She wanted to be alone with Barney as he was so shy. He still hadn't said much; she had done most of the talking. She wanted Barney not to be so shy and to just be himself. Mog Og always did the talking – he could talk all night and all day, and he usually did – but Barney was very mysterious, like the depths of midnight itself. He was very soulful.

All of them sat on the back porch and Mog Og started to sing. The lady cats all joined in – Lady Treacle in her smooth, mellow voice; Cleopatra in her heavenly, sweet voice; and Coconut in her satin, velvet-smooth voice. They sang as the stars twinkled and the full moon hung in the sky and everyone else slept soundly – even the other cats in the neighbourhood slept soundly.

Mog Og woke up. He was still on the back porch at Lady Treacle's place. So he woke up Popcorn and Barney (he gave them a nudge), and they all realised they had to get home before the morning arrived. The girls – Coconut, Cleopatra and Lady Treacle – were still peacefully sleeping, so the boys tiptoed out and headed back down the road known as Kensington Cobbles and through the back streets with a hop, a skip and a jump.

When they were nearly home, they bumped into the alley cats, Katmandu, Beetlejuice, Smokey Joe, Poppy and Pandora. These cats were always outside, prowling around, and they were curious to know where Mog Og had been. The alley cats all had fleas and didn't seem to mind sharing them!

Mog Og piped up: "Watch out, boys! These alley cats have fleas, so let's just say hi to them and then run like the wind. They say they're under the doctor for treatment, but oh boy! It seems to take for ever to get rid of fleas, you know. Poppy and Pandora look very cute, so it's such a shame we can't stop."

The alley cats were too busy scratching their fleas to give chase. They just let Mog Og and his mates whizz off round the corner.

Mog Og was glad he kept a safe distance from the flea-bitten alley cats. He felt so sorry for them, as their fleas made it hard for them to make friends. They were rough diamonds, but they meant well.

George's Secret Compartments

Mog Og finally got home. As he was climbing over the garden fence, he saw Marmalade and Cat Majick dancing and singing under the apple tree. He couldn't believe it. He was a little bit envious, but then he remembered he'd fallen in love with one of the posh cats that he'd just been to see. However, he still wanted to think Marmalade loved him. Luckily she didn't see him, and he quickly ran through the garden and into the house. He got into the kitchen and decided to sleep in the cubbyhole under a tartan rug that was used for picnics. It smelled of French cheese and wine. In no time at all he was fast asleep, dreaming of Coconut.

When he finally woke up, of course he was so hungry, and he went into the kitchen.

Milly noticed him and said, "Where have you been, Mog Og? You've been out for ages. Has anything happened in your world?"

Mog Og yawned. He was still so tired.

"I've had a great evening, Milly, with the posh cats from Hyde Park. Me, Popcorn and Barney met up with Lady Treacle, Cleopatra and Coconut, so we have had an excellent evening. And we're all in love."

"Mog Og," said Milly, "I thought you liked Marmalade."

"Well, I do, Milly, and I like Coconut too. Marmalade was with Cat Majick tonight, and I know Cat Majick has always liked her."

"Oh, I see," said Milly. "It's very complicated in the cat world, isn't it?"

"Well, Milly, I'm going to have another catnap. I've had some milk and I feel a bit refreshed, but I am going to sleep in the hall at the feet of George."

Mog Og went into the hall, and George Midnight, the grandfather clock, was asleep. In fact, he was snoring. His snoring made Mog Og feel tired, so he finally fell asleep at George's feet.

When Mog Og was asleep he couldn't stop thinking about the alley cats with fleas. He so hoped they would get a cure. He actually dreamt that they found a cure, and a few weeks later when he met them (in the dream, of course) they had finally stopped scratching and he could actually make friends with them.

When Mog Og woke up, George was also wide awake, so he had finally stopped snoring.

"George," said Mog Og, "do clocks get fleas or is it just cats?"

"Well, we grandfather clocks are made from mahogany, and we can get woodworm. It riddles our brains with holes. But the good thing is we don't get fleas like cats do."

"Where does mahogany come from?" asked Mog Og.

"It comes from a tree that comes from . . . a M–A–H–O–G–A–N–Y Jungle!"

Mog Og was impressed with George. He seemed to know everything. He also liked to talk to George about Scotland. George told Mog Og about Malaig, the place where he was made, and he told Mog Og about the Loch Ness Monster.

"Have you ever seen the Loch Ness Monster, George?" asked Mog Og.

"Oh, yes. I saw her once. She was sat on a rock near Urquhart Castle, and she was painting her nails red."

"What did she look like?" asked Mog Og. "Did she look like a cat?"

"Well," said George, she looked like a griffin. She had green skin. She looked like a little dragon – like a cute, magical dragon."

"Oh," said Mog Og, "and because she's green they think she's a monster."

"Well," said George, "that's why she was putting nail varnish on her nails: trying to make herself look pretty. When I saw her she looked up and gave me a cute smile."

"So she's actually the Lock Ness Princess, then, George?"

"Well, I would say so," said George. "It's very beautiful, Scotland," said George, "especially the lochs and the glens and the heather. Even though I'm a grandfather clock, I would love to walk out in the open air and visit the lochs and listen to the birds in the trees."

"Yes," said Mog Og, "it sounds lovely. I get sick of Jasmine shouting every ten minutes, Cuckoo! Cuckoo!"

Jasmine Feathersprings, the cuckoo clock, was on the wall in the dining room. Mog Og wasn't so keen on her. They didn't see eye to eye. He'd told her several times to put a sock in it and to shut up. If he slept on the armchair in the dining room she'd suddenly start shouting, "Cuckoo! Cuckoo!" He couldn't understand why she should keep squawking. It made him so mad. Mog Og knew that Milly liked Jasmine and George liked Jasmine, but he had other ideas. He just wanted to shut her up so he could get some sleep. He felt a bit bad about disliking her. The first day she came to the house he was fast asleep in the dining room and suddenly he had been woken so rudely by Jasmine yelling, "Cuckoo! Cuckoo!" Of course she was a cuckoo clock, and that's what cuckoo clocks do. It is how they tell the time, but whenever the cuckoo sprang out yelling, "Cuckoo! Cuckoo!" Mog Og jumped up to try and catch Jasmine.

Jasmine wasn't very happy. She said Mog Og was a very bad-tempered, ugly cat.

That was how Mog Og was first introduced to Jasmine, and it was a bad start. Jasmine had not spoken to Mog Og since. Mog Og wanted to apologise, but Jasmine didn't seem to want to speak to him.

However, she did talk to George a lot – every day, in fact. And she also spoke to Milly every day. In fact Milly was glad that Jasmine was so loud and boisterous. Jasmine was from Cornwall. She was handmade in Tintagel and spoke heartily of Camelot and King Arthur, the Lady of the Lake, Morgana, Guinevere and, of course, Merlin. Jasmine spoke of the Cornish countryside and how relaxing it is.

Mog Og was very interested in Cornwall – it sounded like a place you could get a very deep sleep.

Jasmine believed Cornish pixies existed. She said they dressed in green and danced around mushrooms. Mog Og wondered if pixies like cats. He wanted to meet one. He made a mental note to look for wild mushrooms next time he went on holiday. He hoped the family would go camping in Scotland, rather than Wales, next time.

Then Mog Og fell asleep again, and he dreamt about looking for pixies in Cornwall and looking for the Loch Ness Princess in Scotland. George also fell asleep again. He was snoring.

Milly was talking to Omega Horizon. She was talking about Mog Og going up to the Hyde Park area with Barney and Popcorn and meeting the posh lady cats.

"He's met a lovely lady cat called Coconut," said Milly to Omega Horizon. He seems to be infatuated with her. He says she's very elegant with a lovely voice, but he's worried about the alley cats. They've got fleas and can't stop scratching. He feels so sorry for them."

"George," Milly asked, "is Jasmine feeling OK? She said Mog Og jumped up and tried to pull her feathers off. I think that it is very mean. Mog Og seems concerned about the alley cats, but not about clocks."

"Well," said George, "as you know, cats don't like birds. Because Jasmine is a cuckoo, he isn't very keen on her, Milly."

"Oh, dear!" said Milly. "What do cats actually like, George?"

"Well," said George, "they don't like birds and they don't like water."

"They don't like water!" said Milly. "Well, that is silly. No wonder the alley cats have fleas if they don't like water. I suppose they never have a bath. But Mog Og says he goes dancing in the rain."

"Well," said George, "there are lots of large trees in the garden and he probably dances mostly in the shelter of the large oak trees. If he doesn't dance in the shade of the trees, he must be a very unusual cat, as they generally don't like water."

"Aren't cats strange?" said Milly. "They don't like water and they don't like birds, and they sleep most of the time and then go out at midnight."

"Oh, yes," said George. "In Egypt, cats are worshipped. There is a cat goddess called Bastet, and there are lots of cats in Egypt."

"What's Egypt like, George?"

"Well, it's very hot, there's lots of sand and there's pyramids and temples and pharaohs."

"I bet Mog Og would love Egypt – especially if it's hot."

"Oh, George, what exactly are scarecrows? I heard Mog Og saying he is going to fetch the scarecrows to Jasmine."

George started to laugh – a deep hearty laugh – until tears streamed from his eyes.

"Oh, that is so mean of Mog Og to say he's fetching the scarecrows to scare poor Jasmine to death."

"What are they?" said Milly, feeling worried about an army of scarecrows coming to the house.

"Well," said George, "they are mostly made to scare

birds from fields. They are like people, but they have straw for hair, a carrot for a nose and nothing for a brain. They usually wear someone else's clothes. They are quite scary, but they can't walk or run very far, and I think they are scared of cats as cats can bite their trouser legs."

"But I don't think an army of scarecrows will be on their way. I think it's Mog Og being a bit mean, but I'll have a word with Jasmine and settle her mind. I'll also tell Mog Og to tell any scarecrows on their way here to go back to Cornwall."

"Oh, George," said Milly, "you are a diamond. I think if you talk to Mog Og, he'll realise he's being a bit mean."

Then suddenly Milly heard George snoring. He was having an afternoon nap.

Milly was very impressed with how much George knew. He seemed to know everything about history and geography. George had studied hard at clock school, and he had gained a masters degree. He had a secret compartment at the back of the clock, which contained manuscripts about the history of the world. George had read them all several times, but no one else had ever read them. He had another secret compartment, and this one held a time viewer which could be used to view scenes in history. So George Midnight was indeed very knowledgeable, as all the other clocks had found out — and they were all very impressed.

Mabble Merlin's Delivery Van

It was almost time for Penelope's birthday cocktail party. Patrick had bought the picture clock, London Melody, and he was keen to have it delivered in time.

Patrick informed Miles that the delivery of London Melody was due for that day. Miles said to Patrick that he would keep an eye out for the delivery van. Miles wasn't going out that day so he was sure he would hear the doorbell.

Meanwhile, early that morning, Mabble Merlin loaded up the delivery van. He had a lot of things to deliver. He had to go to Pluckley, a village near Ashford in Kent, and he also had to go to Eastbourne.

Mabble Merlin loaded the van up. It was a 1940s-style delivery van. It was black with gold trimmings and gold signwriting in the shape of an arch, which looked rather artistic and eye-catching. It read, 'The Musty Old Magical Curiosity Shop'.

Mabble Merlin jumped into the van and sped off. His first stop was the home of Dr and Mrs Laugherty in Bayswater. He wove in and out of the early morning rush-hour traffic, which was almost bumper-to-bumper; it didn't take him long at all. Soon enough he was at Dr and Mrs Laugherty's house.

He admired the nice porch on the front of the house. It was one of these large Victorian town houses with a nice stained-glass door. He pressed the doorbell.

Miles rushed to the door and glimpsed the delivery van speeding off down the avenue; and he saw that there was a very large parcel left inside the porch. He picked it up and noticed it was addressed to 'Penelope Laugherty', so he guessed it was Penelope's birthday present. He brought it in and put it on the bottom shelf of the closet in the hallway. The picture was wrapped in deep-blue shiny wrapping paper, tied with a light-blue bow.

Mabble Merlin was now on his way to Pluckley, where he was delivering a gold antique mirror to a couple that owned the Lion and Unicorn Inn. They had recently bought the inn and were renovating it.

The village of Pluckley was said to be haunted, and they were sure the inn was haunted. They had strange goings-on in the inn – and it would get a lot stranger once the mirror was delivered. One morning, as they lay in bed, the landlord said to his wife, "Wouldn't it be funny if we woke up one morning and found ourselves in another house, or another inn, somewhere else completely!"

Mabble Merlin had decided to drive down the country lanes towards Kent. He was speeding along. It was so easy to drive the van: he just had to put his hands on the steering wheel and it drove itself. So he had plenty of time to view the countryside. He pressed a button and the van whizzed down the winding country lanes so fast it became a blur. The cows in the fields stopped chewing the cud and looked up to see what it was, and in one field all the sheep started running about. All the animals knew they were witnessing something strange. The delivery van reached warp speed!

Mabble Merlin arrived in Pluckley and delivered the antique mirror to the Lion and Unicorn Inn. The inn was about 500 years old. He walked into the inn and handed over the mirror.

"Oh, thank you," the landlord said.

He and his wife were both serving behind the bar. They

both thought Mabble Merlin was dressed strangely. He had a beret on and a long trench coat and a long scarf that was wrapped round his neck several times. It was the longest scarf they ever saw. In fact, they wondered how he walked without tripping over it. They looked out of the window and saw the old delivery van, and when they looked back to where Mabble Merlin had been standing he wasn't there; he was already back in the delivery van!

The young inn owners, Sally and Richard Knight, rushed outside, but the strange delivery man and van were gone. They looked at the antique mirror and looked at each other and realised it wasn't going to be an ordinary mirror. All they knew was that their aunt had bought it for them from an antique shop in London as a house-warming present. They had invited their aunt to visit them at the inn in the summertime, when the renovation work was completed. Their Aunt Lydia had bought several other things from the antique shop – she thought they would be suitable for the inn.

Mabble Merlin was now driving at warp speed down the winding country lanes of Kent. He was going to the Queen's Head Hotel in Eastbourne, where he had an antique bed to deliver.

When he arrived at the hotel the receptionist was astonished because she didn't hear him walking across the tiled floor. Mabble Merlin suddenly seemed to appear.

"I've come to deliver a bed," he told her.

The hotel porter helped Mabble Merlin to bring in the bed. The bed was from the 1840s yet it looked brand new.

The porter asked, "Is this a reproduction? It looks brand new."

"It's not a reproduction – it's the real thing."

The hotelier arrived and helped with the bed.

Mabble Merlin said, "That's a very special bed. You certainly will enjoy a good night's sleep in it."

"It looks brand new," said the hotelier, Philip Chase, but there's a label on here that says '1840 – Handmade by Bedknobs and Broomsticks of Bristol'.

Philip looked up at Mabble Merlin.

"It is brand new," said Mabble Merlin. "It's never been used."

"Oh," said Philip, "I see."

Philip was bemused.

Suddenly he was distracted when the receptionist told him that seven guests had missed an organised trip to the medieval town of Rye and Beachy Head, which is not far from Eastbourne. The coach had left without them.

Mabble Merlin offered to take the guests to Beachy Head and Rye, and also to Camber Castle, once owned by Henry VIII, not far from the nature reserve.

The seven guests all bundled into the van – and there were plenty of seats for them; the seats tucked away when it was used as a delivery van.

With the seven guests in the van, Mabble Merlin drove off down the road towards Beachy Head. The van raced along the leafy lanes at warp speed. While the van drove itself, Mabble Merlin was able to turn to the hotel guests and have a conversation with them. They thought he must know the area like the back of his hand, not to have to keep looking at the road.

Finally the van came to a grinding halt, and they all got out and breathed in the beautiful sea air. Below them were the jade-green sea and the white chalky cliffs of Beachy Head.

Mabble Merlin told the hotel guests that there were tunnels inside the cliffs, where hobbits and leprechauns and hobgoblins lived. He told them that the caves were lined with gemstones like amethyst.

Suddenly the seven hotel guests found themselves in a gemstone cavern. The floor of the cavern was made from black obsidian and there was a table and chairs made from obsidian. They all sat on the seats. Mabble Merlin sat on a very tall chair. It was made from a gemstone called obsidian snowflake, which is black with splodges of white – the same sort of white as the chalky cliffs. The seven hotel guests looked at one another and felt very relaxed and peaceful.

Then in trundled what looked like a leprechaun. He was dressed all in green. He offered the seven hotel guests a cup of tea and biscuits.

They drank the tea and ate the biscuits, and Mabble Merlin told them about the little people that lived in the caves. Then Mabble Merlin said it was time they were going, and they walked up a gemstone staircase made from obsidian.

In no time at all they reached the top of the staircase, where there was an opening in the top of the cliffs. They all walked out into the sunlight and found themselves back at the very spot they had started from, overlooking the jade-green sea. When they looked back, the entrance to the caves had disappeared.

Then Mabble Merlin shouted, "Hurry up! We're all going to the ancient medieval town of Rye."

They all got into the van and fastened their seat belts, and Mabble Merlin drove helter-skelter along the winding cliffs and the winding, narrow country roads. He held the steering wheel of the van and turned to talk to the guests. They noticed he never looked at the road once. He chatted to them calmly and casually. After the experience of being in the gemstone cave, and being given tea and biscuits by a leprechaun, they knew that Mabble Merlin was stranger than fiction; so they listened to everything he had to say, staring into his mud-brown eyes.

In no time at all they reached Rye. Rye is a delightful place with a church from the twelfth century.

The hotel guests were Karl and Evie from London, Clive and Corrine from Morecambe, Kate and Harry from Beccles near Lowestoft, and Roger from Cardiff. They were all really enjoying the trip with Mabble Merlin. When they got to Rye, they wanted to go to one of the taverns up the cobbled streets of the steep Mint, as it is called. They went into the Mermaid Tavern, where they all had the chef's special: 'Smuggler's pie' with chips. Basically, this is fish pie with vegetables and mushrooms. The chef came out to ask them if they had enjoyed it. He looked very trendy, and they noticed his ginger hair looked very stylish. His chef's outfit was tailor-made and high fashion. He asked what sweet they would like, and he recommended the ginger pudding and custard – perhaps because his hair was ginger! It had real ginger in it. The chef's name was Rex Mahoney. He came from Ireland, and he certainly knew how to cook. The pudding was delicious. They also ordered Irish coffee, and cheese and biscuits, and Mabble Merlin entertained them with all kinds of stories about his shop, which they all promised to visit whenever they were in London. He gave them his business card so they wouldn't forget.

At last it was time for Mabble Merlin to take them back to the Queen's Head Hotel in Eastbourne. They all boarded the van and fastened their seat belts. Mabble Merlin took hold of the steering wheel and zoom! They whizzed at great speed along the narrow winding country lanes. Chickens in their chicken coops flew off their perches in alarm when the van whizzed past faster than the speed of sound. The hens certainly laid a few more eggs than usual that day! The cockerel started squawking his head off. A farmer and his wife in the sleepy village of Baldslow looked out of their window to see the black-and-gold 40s-style van whizzing past as if it wasn't touching the road. Faster and faster went the van, but Mabble Merlin still managed to talk to the hotel guests without looking at the road even once. The seven of them were talking fast to him, and he was talking just as fast to all of them. In fact, everything was speeded up.

When they arrived in Eastbourne, the guests got out of the van and quickly walked up the steps of the Queen's Head Hotel. Philip Chase was waiting for them to arrive. They were all in a good mood. Mabble Merlin waved goodbye and the guests waved back and thanked him for a most amazing trip.

The Sound of Running Water

The hotelier asked if they had enjoyed the trip with Mabble Merlin, and they all said it was fabulous and they wouldn't have missed it for the world. They were all so tired that they all went straight to their hotel rooms. Roger was in Room 13. He had arrived at the hotel late and hadn't previously checked into the room because it hadn't been ready. While he was on the trip with Mabble Merlin the new bed had been moved into his room, so when he opened the door of the room he saw the antique bed for the first time. It looked like a bed fit for a king!

Roger had brought his laptop with him, intending to do some work on tracing his family tree. Some of his ancestors had originated from the south of England; and he wanted to go to Rye, where one of his ancestors had been a smuggler. He had put his name down for the Rye Ghost Walk. Rye had captured his imagination. He had enjoyed the day trip to Rye. Now he planned to spend a few days in Eastbourne and a few days in Brighton and then spend a week in Rye.

He took out his laptop and sat at the desk in the bedroom. On the Internet he found a nice hotel in Brighton and he looked at possible hotels in Rye. He booked an online reservation in Brighton at the Sahara Hotel, which included a Beachcomber Restaurant, a Sand Shuffle Bar and a Blue Nile Cocktail Lounge. He also booked an online reservation at the Smuggler's Tavern, which included the Smuggler's Cove Cocktail Bar and the Blue Lagoon Lounge. He was really pleased with his choice of reservations.

He made himself a cup of hot chocolate and was ready for a good night's sleep in the antique bed that had just been bought from the Musty Old Magical Curiosity Shop. He got into the antique bed, and he dreamt about the Sand Shuffle Bar. The Sand Shuffle Bar had a sand-coloured voile curtain along one wall, and, to the sounds of desert music, a cinema screen appeared showing a desert scene. Three camels moved across the scene, and then the music stopped and the sand-coloured curtain closed.

Roger was a restaurant manager in Cardiff. He was interested in the pub trade and hotels because he was hoping one day to buy a property somewhere on the south coast, so he planned to do a bit of market research during his holiday. He was sceptical about ghosts, but he was curious! He didn't actually believe everything that had happened that day with Mabble Merlin. He thought it was a set-up or Mabble Merlin was a hypnotist. He had noticed Mabble Merlin had strange hypnotic owl eyes. Before he went to sleep he made up his mind that in the morning he would type up his experiences on his laptop. Then he thought he might have a walk along the beach of Eastbourne to clear his mind.

The antique bed had a richly ornate hand-carved headboard and a rich mulberry satin quilt. The mattress was so comfortable that he had fallen asleep immediately.

He hadn't been asleep long when he woke up abruptly to the sound of running water. The sound seemed to be coming from inside the bed. He thought for a split second that he'd had too much hot chocolate to drink the night before, and he jumped up out of bed fearing he'd had a little accident. The bed sheet was soaking wet. He felt embarrassed that he'd wet the bed, and he thought, 'How very odd!' He went to the wardrobe to see if there was a spare sheet.

There were spare blankets, but no sheets. He was feeling suddenly so tired that he decided to get back into the bed and the next thing he knew it was morning. He looked at the sheets and felt that they were dry, so he concluded that he must have dreamt the whole thing, but he remembered how real it seemed.

He had a nice walk along the beach, and then he went for breakfast. He felt rather relieved that the bed was dry and that the sound of running water seemed to have been in his imagination after all.

The Lucky Charm Bracelet

It was a few weeks before Penelope's birthday, and Daisy and Oliver wanted to buy their mum a present. So one Saturday morning they decided to go into Kensington and to take a short cut through Hyde Park. Miles went with the children. He wanted to buy some silverware for the birthday party, as well as some crockery and some table linen that would look suitable for a 1920s-themed party. There was a shop in Kensington called The Silver Spoon, and Miles wanted to go and browse around it.

It was a pleasant day when they arrived in Kensington and walked along one of the busy streets lined with restaurants. Suddenly they came to an opening that led down a cobbled back alley that they hadn't noticed before – at least Miles hadn't noticed it before. There was a billboard in the back alley on the cobblestones that read, 'Eye-catching silver jewellery, silver tableware, 1920s crockery and 1920s Irish table linen'. Miles couldn't believe it. It was as if someone had read his mind. Halfway down the cobbled street, tucked out of sight, there was an antique shop. There were several steps up to the shop, and it was so narrow and quaint with a small bow window. A quaint shop sign hung above the door: 'Welcome to the Musty Old Magical Curiosity Shop'.

Miles was so excited. He believed he would find everything he wanted in this shop. He had been in a shop like this a few weeks before in the Bayswater area, he thought there must be more than one Musty Old Magical Curiosity Shop. The shopkeeper looked rather different, so Miles didn't think they were the same person.

"How can I help you today?" asked Mabble Merlin.

"Well, I'm looking for some silver tableware – knives, forks, spoons, sugar bowl, salt and pepper pots and a milk jug. I would also like a silver tray and some table linen. We're having a 1920s-themed cocktail party – a birthday party."

"That's wonderful!" said Mabble Merlin. "Now come over here. I've got everything you need and more."

Mabble Merlin handed Miles a leather box, and Miles opened it. It contained the most exquisite silver tableware. Miles picked out a silver spoon and turned it over to look at the maker's mark. It had been made in Boston, USA, in 1923, so it was perfect for the 1920s-themed party. Miles was very pleased with the silverware.

Mabble Merlin brought out another leather box, containing a silver milk jug, sugar bowl, tray, and salt and pepper pots. These were all made in Virginia, USA, in 1922.

All that Miles needed now was the table linen. Before Miles could say anything, Mabble Merlin had handed him a bale of linen.

"That's the best Irish linen that we have," said Mabble Merlin.

Miles looked at the label on the linen. It read, 'Made in County Cork, Ireland, in 1925'.

"That's just perfect," said Miles, "just perfect."

"Now, how can I help you two children?" said Mabble Merlin. "What are you looking for?"

Daisy piped up: "We're looking for a piece of jewellery for Mum's birthday."

Mabble Merlin pulled a beautiful trinket box from a glass cabinet and opened it up to reveal a silver charm bracelet. They all just looked at it; they were all speechless.

"This, I think, would make a beautiful gift," said Mabble Merlin.

Mabble Merlin placed it on the shop counter. The charm bracelet had seven silver charms: a heart-shaped locket, a dice, a pixie, a key, a miniature locket watch, a horseshoe and a fairy. Mabble Merlin explained to the children that all the lucky charms were very lucky indeed, and they all had a magic of their own. Mabble Merlin explained that the miniature locket watch could help the owner to get into the kingdom of the little people. The owner of the charm bracelet had to find out how each of the charms worked; Mabble Merlin couldn't tell them. He could only say that each charm had a different lucky power.

The children were very impressed with the charm bracelet.

"It's really pretty," said Daisy to Mabble Merlin.

"Yes, it's very eye-catching, and I don't think your mum will be disappointed."

He then popped it into a gold trinket box, placed it in a gold satin bag and handed it to Daisy. Daisy was over the moon with it. She thought it was a delightful gift.

Oliver piped up: "I think we should buy something else for Mum, to go with the bracelet."

Mabble Merlin handed Oliver a gift voucher.

"Here is a gift voucher for the Magical Mystery Tour – a holiday for two. It can be for a week or longer, and the destination is a secret."

"That sounds exciting," said Oliver. "I'll definitely take that."

"That's an excellent suggestion," said Daisy.

"Well, you won't be disappointed, because it will be out of this world."

Mabble Merlin wasn't exaggerating – all Mabble Merlin's trips were beyond the imagination.

Mabble Merlin was wearing a 1920s suit with spats, a waistcoat and a bow tie.

Suddenly Miles piped up: "Where did you get the suit?"

Mabble Merlin turned to a corner of the shop and pointed to a rack of 1920s clothes that Miles hadn't noticed before. He flicked through the selection of 1920s suits and dresses, accessories and shoes. He was sure that the forty-eight guests coming to the party would want to be dressed in outfits like these. Miles pulled the guest list out of his pocket and he was pleased to find that there were suits and dresses for everyone. The clothes looked brand new, and they had all been designed by the most famous 1920s designers.

Mabble Merlin piped up: "If you leave a list of the names of people attending the party, we'll have their names sewn into their outfits, and we'll have them specially delivered with shoes and accessories to match. Leave it to me, Miles. I'll enjoy very much choosing their outfits."

Miles had intended going to an exclusive vintage-clothing shop in Oxford Street, but these clothes were perfect. They seemed so expensive and exclusive-looking!

Miles just thought, 'Gosh! This is going to be such an exciting 1920s party. The guests will be delighted.'

Mabble Merlin's Business Card

Miles and the children were very pleased with their purchases. They had purchased everything they needed in one shop.

Miles decided it was time for some lunch, and he knew the perfect place: a restaurant in Kensington High Street called The Pecan Pie. It was very popular. It sold organic wholefoods and had large wooden tables and a stone floor. Some of the food was on display.

Miles and the children went into the restaurant and sat down at one of the large wooden tables. Miles decided to have chilli con carne with brown rice; Daisy decided to have seafood pizza with prawns, crayfish and pineapple; and Oliver chose pasta twists sprinkled with poppy seeds, with yellowfin tuna, baby sweetcorn, courgettes, mangetout and tomato sauce with basil.

As Miles and Daisy and Oliver waited for their food to arrive, they sipped organic fruit juices. Miles had pineapple, mango and ginger, and the children had strawberry and cherry. They were served with coloured straws, fancy cocktail umbrellas and a slice of lime each. As they drank their organic fruit juices they had another look at the goods they had just bought. Daisy took out the silver charm bracelet. She was wondering what each charm could do. Miles was looking at the silverware.

When the waitress, Emily, arrived, she admired the utterly beautiful charm bracelet and asked where they had purchased it.

Miles piped up that it was a small shop just down the side street with a billboard on view.

Emily said she had been along that street many times, but had never ever seen that shop. She said she thought it must have just opened. She told them she was thinking of buying a necklace to replace her favourite one, which she had recently lost.

Meanwhile, as if by magic or telepathy, Mabble Merlin popped out of the shop and on the billboard on the cobblestones he chalked the words 'Silver gemstone necklaces – choose from rose quartz, amethyst, blue lace agate, clear quartz, moonstone, jasper, aventurine and obsidian'. He seemed to know that Emily was going to pop into the shop.

When Emily finished work she easily found the shop down the side street, and she bought a heart-shaped rose-quartz silver necklace. From then on she wore the necklace every day, and the customers in The Pecan Pie often commented on how beautiful it was, but none of the customers ever found the shop – and, curiously enough, Emily never saw the shop again. She thought it was very strange that the shop was suddenly there and suddenly gone.

The Musty Old Magical Curiosity Shop could make itself invisible if it wanted to. The owl in the shop window, Hoot-Hoot, sometimes stared into a would-be customer's eyes, and if he didn't think that person was ready to buy anything magical from the shop, he would make the would-be customer feel so, so, so sleepy. Some of these would-be customers went straight home without buying any of the things they went into town for, and all they could remember was seeing an owl in a shop window. Sometimes would-be customers went into the shop and the owl handed them a business card and then hypnotised them with his large owl eyes to go home and put their feet up. Hours later the would-be customers would wake up at home holding a business card which read: 'You have had an encounter with the Musty Old Magical Curiosity Shop. Don't call us, we'll call you. Proprietor: Mabble Merlin, at your service.' The card was purple with silver writing and a few strange symbols, which looked like very ancient magic symbols. The people would look at the card for a long time wondering where on earth the Musty Old Magical Curiosity Shop actually was. They often waited eagerly for the call, but for many of them the call never came.

Milly Paris Gets to Know Polly Quazar

Penelope opened her present from Miles and was very pleased with the very quaint Australian clock. She loved it.

Polly Quazar, the sweet Australian clock, was put above the mantelpiece in the dining room. As she was telepathic she had no trouble talking to Milly Paris — which she did, morning, noon and night. They chatted for hours, mostly about Australia and about the Aboriginal Dreamtime. Milly was so fascinated by it.

One day disaster struck. Milly's hands stopped working. She had just put on her favourite fragrance, Paris Time, and was feeling very happy, when Polly whispered to Milly that it was nine o'clock exactly. Milly's hands spun round and round, but the spinning wore the mechanism and suddenly one of the hands got stuck at eight o'clock. Milly struggled to turn the hands to nine o'clock, but to no avail. They simply wouldn't budge. She strained and strained, but still nothing happened. She started to sob.

"Oh dear, oh dear, oh dear!" she cried.

Mog Og strolled into the kitchen.

"Oh, Milly, do stop sobbing. Dry your eyes. Your perfume, Paris Time, is lovely and sweet and Polly is your friend. What's got into you? I'll go and get you a handkerchief so you can dry your eyes."

"I – I – I can't move my hands to nine o'clock, Mog Og. All the spinning and whirring of my hands has broken the mechanism. I am doomed. Doomed! Doomed!" she wailed.

Polly, in the next room, could hear her cries.

"Milly, whatever is the matter, my dear friend? Has Mog Og upset you, or are you suffering from a chill or the flu, with the English weather?"

Polly always thought the wet English weather was responsible for everyone being a little bit temperamental in England.

"No, Polly. My hands are stuck. If I push my hands any more, they will drop off. I have been whizzing my hands round and round and round, guessing the time and trying to catch up with all of you lot. I'm not much use. I'm as good as a chocolate Advent clock."

A chocolate clock isn't much use for telling the time, that is true.

"I know Dr Laugherty will just put me on a dusty shelf in the dusty attic."

Polly interrupted with her keen Aboriginal insight: "I think you're right, Milly. He's sure to do just that."

"Oh, oh, oh!" wailed Milly.

"But wait – I haven't finished," piped up Polly. "I can see you getting better and coming back so much happier. I'm certain of it. You'll see – it will happen, so don't be sad."

Milly continued to sob, and Mog Og offered her a handkerchief. Her mascara was ruined and her lipstick was smudged. Mog Og felt very sorry for her. He jumped on to a chair and stretched up and wiped her face clean so she could put on some more mascara and pink lipstick and put a bit of rouge on her cheeks as she looked so pale. Milly realised crying wouldn't help, so at last she fell silent and dried her tears.

Mog Og began to sing, just to cheer Milly up:

"Milly, Milly, you're like a fresh Paris flower in springtime.
You're too nice, too sweet to hide away on a dusty shelf
I'm gonna make a wish that you stay
And hope you don't sob all day,
So smile your pretty clock smile
And start to sway."

Milly was glad that Mog Og was singing. It cheered her up, and she soon felt everything would somehow be fine, even though she thought it was the worst time of her life. It was rather bitter-sweet because she had some good friends – especially Jasmine and Polly and George and Mog Og. She'd also heard that a new picture clock had arrived named London Melody. It wasn't yet on the wall, but she was looking forward to meeting it.

A Trip to the Seaside

Every year the Laugherty family liked to take a trip to the Jurassic Coast in Dorset.

In Jurassic rocks you may find, if you are extremely lucky, dinosaur bones; and if you are really imaginative, you can glimpse the long-distant past – the age of the dinosaurs, when dinosaurs like *Tyrannosaurus rex* roamed the earth, and pterodactyls flew in the skies.

So one weekend the family arrived in Weymouth after a long car journey from London, and they headed for the picturesque harbour, where fishing boats bobbed about and yachts lay moored.

They decided to go to the Renaissance Fayre, where everyone was in full sixteenth-century costume, recreating the atmosphere of the Tudor era. Musicians were playing Tudor music, and many of the people at the fayre seemed to have actually come straight from the sixteenth century. In fact, some of the musicians from the fayre had actually time-travelled from sixteenth-century London.

As well as the fayre, something else had showed up unexpectedly. Guess what it was! Well, it was the Musty Old Magical Curiosity Shop, and it was sandwiched between a palmist's shop and a seashell shop. The palmist was a Romany gypsy named Clara May Lee, who had already foretold that the curiosity shop would turn up on the day of the Renaissance Fayre. The seashell shop was named The Sea Urchin. This sold beach balls, buckets, spades, sunglasses, surfboards and, of course, seashells, including huge conch shells and nautilus shells.

The Laugherty family strolled happily along the Esplanade eating fish and chips, while the sea breezes blew away the cobwebs of care. They had not a care in the world. However, poor Milly's world was about to turn upside down.

Before long the Laugherty family noticed the palmist's shop, and Penelope was very eager to go into the shop to get her palm read. At that moment Patrick suddenly noticed the Musty Old Magical Curiosity Shop next to the palmist's. He couldn't believe it. It looked exactly like the musty old shop he'd been into down a side street in Kensington. He was amazed that the two shops looked so similar. Patrick wandered in, but this time Mabble Merlin was dressed in sixteenth-century costume. He looked like a writer from Tudor times. He wore a black velvet cloth cap with a large purple feather, a purple-and-gold waistcoat, a very flamboyant white frilly cotton shirt, black leggings, and black pointed shoes with gold buckles. His hair was long and dark, and he had a black moustache and beard. On the shop counter there was a very large book filled with Mabble Merlin's writings.

Mabble Merlin loved to write, and indeed he had many things to write about. He wrote about his customers and his travels, his journeys and his thoughts on life. Some of his stories were incredible.

Patrick noticed that the shopkeeper's eyes were the same mud-brown colour as the eyes of the shopkeeper in Kensington.

Suddenly Mabble Merlin piped up: "How can I help you, sir?"

"Oh, erm, I'm looking for a kitchen clock actually. The one we have has unfortunately broken; its hands have stuck, you see."

"Now, do come over here, sir. I've something perfect for you – and I think you'll agree."

Penelope, Daisy and Oliver were now standing in the shop. Penelope had decided she wanted to buy a necklace for the 1920s-themed cocktail party. Penelope didn't know that Mabble Merlin had all of the outfits and accessories for the cocktail party ready to be delivered. There were feather boas, headbands, necklaces and bracelets for the ladies. However, Mabble Merlin had known that Penelope would be popping into the shop to choose her own accessories – and he was never wrong!

Penelope went over to the jewellery shelf and opened a beautiful silver trinket box. Inside there was a very eye-catching silver and gemstone necklace. On the end of the silver chain was a pyramid-shaped lapis-lazuli gemstone. It had been fashioned in the time of the Ancient Egyptians. It was truly mesmerising. There was also a lapis-lazuli bracelet with little gemstone pyramids. It had a regal look about it.

As she opened the silver trinket box, Penelope somehow felt that these items of jewellery had been made for the wife of Tutankhamen, Ankhsenamun, who was Queen of Egypt over 3,000 years ago. Penelope felt an immediate connection with the necklace, and Mabble Merlin informed her that it was indeed worn by the Egyptian queen. Patrick immediately offered to buy the jewellery. It was perfect for his queen, Penelope.

Mabble Merlin popped the Egyptian jewellery back into the trinket box, wrapped it all in gold wrapping paper, popped it into a gold satin bag and handed it to Penelope. It made Penelope feel so elegant and regal to know she had a 3,000-year-old necklace and bracelet that once belonged to an Ancient Egyptian queen.

Patrick was then shown a French kitchen clock, which had once belonged to Marie Antoinette and Louis XVI. It was given to them as a wedding present.

Marie Antoinette loved beautiful things, and the people of France loved her very much, but one day when she was feeling a bit spiteful, and more worried about her hair than the people of France, someone asked her, "What shall we eat?"

She replied, "Let them eat cake."

Unfortunately she was carted off somewhere to be beheaded, and the French clock, Claudette de Seconds, somehow ended up in the Musty Old Magical Curiosity Shop along with most of Marie Antoinette's clothes and other artefacts from the royal palace. Louis XVI met the same fate as his wife. They were rather unforgiving, the French. Well, Marie Antoinette lived in an age when French ladies wore white wigs, and brightly coloured taffeta dresses with satin and lace. They always looked very grand. They danced and wrote lovely poetry.

Well, Claudette de Seconds was now in Weymouth on the Dorset coast.

Dr Laugherty held the clock. He liked this pink and pompous kitchen clock with the face of Marie Antoinette painted in a cameo in the centre of the clock. In the portrait she was eating cake – a lovely strawberry-and-cream cake. The clock was extraordinary. It had the magical ability to record things, and it contained a record of everything that had happened at the French court. Claudette de Seconds was a very good historian. If the Laugherty children needed to know about life at the French court, then Claudette de Seconds could chatter about that to their hearts' content. She could tell them all about the fancy white wigs that they wore and the powdered ladies with beautiful satin puffed-out dresses and silver-buckled shoes. The ladies often carried satin parasols and spent their time painting in the courtyards or walking in the gardens, which were scented with the fragrance of roses, lilacs, lavender and vanilla. It was an easy, storybook life at the court (unless of course you told everyone to shut up and eat cake – then you got into big trouble, like Queen Marie Antoinette).

Cough Castle

"Yes, yes, I'll take this," said Dr Laugherty.

He purchased the French clock, and Mabble Merlin wrapped it in beautiful pink wrapping paper and tied it with a pink bow. He then popped it into a pink satin bag.

Dr Laugherty, Penelope and the children left the shop. Dr Laugherty had planned a special treat for Daisy and Oliver: they travelled from Weymouth along the coast to the Isle of Purbeck, where they all went on the Swanage Steam Railway. They took a trip to Cough Castle, not far from the town of Swanage.

They sat in a little old compartment of the steam train as it huffed and puffed along the tracks. The train was just like the Orient Express. The steam train was named the Dorset Choo-Choo. The steam train went through tiny villages en route, but the scenery was mainly farmland, with sheep and cows and horses and occasional pigsties. The cows in the fields turned their heads and wondered what on earth was going past them and giving off a lot of hot air. They looked so surprised! The poor little sheep (who get nervous if a sheep dog runs after them) started running up the hill in one field, and the pigs stopped eating their pigswill to look up to see what the great monstrosity was.

Oliver and Daisy had a great time waving to the children that lived in the little villages. They poked their heads out of the cottage windows and waved back at the train. Even some Dorset scarecrows waved back at the children. Oliver and Daisy felt like royalty.

When the steam train eventually came to a halt, Patrick said, "I've got another surprise: we're now going to Cough Castle."

They all got off the train at a little village named Church Knowle, where a signpost told them it was a five-minute walk to the castle.

Patrick had already made a booking for the family to stay the night at the castle, but the family didn't know they had a room booked. They hadn't even known the castle existed before that day. For that matter, they hadn't known the Dorset Choo-Choo existed either.

The day was getting better and better. Oliver loved castles. He wanted to own a castle when he grew up. He thought he might renovate an old ruined castle – and there are plenty of those. There is even a ruined castle on the outskirts of London, in nearby Hertfordshire – South Mimms Castle. Oliver thought ruined castles *should* be renovated, and that was his ambition.

When they had walked for about five minutes they suddenly came upon Cough Castle. Oliver was transported back in time. He imagined it in days gone by with a moat and a drawbridge. He imagined himself as a knight, walking up to the castle.

They all went inside the castle, where there was a large display that told the history of the castle. The staff were all dressed in period costume, and a few of them were dressed like knights. The lights were dimmed to give the effect of a haunted castle. At first visitors cannot see clearly in the gloomy room, but their eyes soon adjust to the dark.

One of the staff, dressed in a cook's outfit, suddenly said, "Hello, Patrick."

Penelope said to Patrick, "How did she know your name?"

"I have no idea," said Patrick. "Maybe it was a ghost."

When they turned back, the cook was gone.

Then something touched Penelope's face, and she screamed. But it was only the pretend cobwebs in the corner of the wall.

Then one of the knights whispered to Oliver, "Welcome to Cough Castle, Oliver."

Penelope turned and said, "How does he know your name?"

Oliver lifted the knight's helmet, but there was nothing inside – certainly no person!

Then suddenly the lights came on. They had been watching the Haunted Cough Castle Show, and now everything looked very charming. The waitress came over and offered them tea and biscuits in the castle lounge, and they gratefully accepted. The lounge was all wood-panelled with a wooden floor and large wooden tables and chairs. The family sat down to enjoy their tea and biscuits.

As Daisy was eating a biscuit, out of the corner of her eye she glimpsed a girl the same age as her with hair in ringlets. She was carrying a rag doll in one hand, and some books in the other hand. She walked towards the bookcase, where she pressed a button. The bookcase swung away from the wall and she walked through. It was as if she was deliberately showing Daisy a secret passageway in the castle.

"That's so cool!" said Daisy.

"What's so cool?" said Oliver.

Daisy explained to Oliver what she had seen.

"That doesn't surprise me," said Oliver matter-of-factly. "There is always, always a secret passageway in a castle like this."

"Well, children," said Patrick, "I have made a booking for us to stay the night. I think we all deserve a break in a haunted castle."

They all laughed so much that the staff wondered what

was so funny. In fact, a waiter came over and asked them why they were laughing.

"It's just the fact that this castle's haunted," said Patrick.

"Oh, you like it, then?" said the waiter, and he grabbed a white tablecloth, put it over his head and went "Whoo! Whoo!"

"How haunted is this place?" asked Penelope.

She thought she could use the story for the magazine she wrote for: *Paranormal Investigations*.

"Well," said the waiter, whose name was Jack Rose, "it's supposed to be haunted by a cook named Annie Shoreditch, a knight named Henry Bodenham, and a young girl named Ella Louise Levens. Some people say they have seen them all."

"Goodness me!" exclaimed Penelope.

Daisy just looked at Oliver. They realised they had seen all three of the ghosts within minutes of being in the castle. They found it very exciting.

Jack Rose took them all upstairs to their rooms. When he opened the door of Patrick and Ponelope's room, they were astounded. The floor was transparent, so they could see the people below in the lounge.

"Don't worry," said Jack Rose, "it's only transparent one way; they can't see you."

"Where is the bed?" said Patrick.

"It is tucked away in the wall."

"It's very modern for a castle," said Penelope.

Then Jack Rose flicked a switch, and suddenly the old-looking floorboards of the castle reappeared and the bed lowered down from out of the wall.

"Actually," said Jack Rose, "the transparent floor is just an optical illusion – a hologram. The owner of the castle designs holographic images and optical illusions."

The owners of Cough Castle were Lord and Lady Smedley-Barrington.

Then Jack Rose flicked yet another switch, and on the back wall of the room there was suddenly a scene of a battle going on, with knights on horses and soldiers in battledress. It looked so real. Jack Rose flicked another switch and the screen showed the moat around the castle, where a celebration was taking place. It looked like a medieval party. The drawbridge was down and the celebration party was taking place on the bridge itself. The scene reminded Patrick of King Arthur and the knights of Camelot. One of the ladies looked like Queen Guinevere.

Jack Rose flicked another switch and the hotel room was back to normal – as normal as it ever would be. Patrick and Penelope thought it was fantastic.

Then Jack Rose showed them all Daisy and Oliver's room, which contained a little alcove with a bunk bed in it. There were tartan blankets on the beds. Jack Rose flicked a switch and the bunk bed moved. It went up, up to the ceiling, but it could also move sideways or it could move as if it was on a merry-go-round. The room was almost circular. In the middle of the floor was a transparent area, and, on the far side of the alcove where the bunk bed was, a doorway led to a balcony.

Jack Rose flicked another switch, and in the middle of the floor a huge eye appeared. From the pupil of the eye a huge tube-shaped object popped up, and other tubes appeared from the centre of the first tube. These tubes grew longer and longer until they joined to the bunk bed.

"What on earth are those tubes?" asked Patrick.

"It's a chute," said Jack Rose. "It leads to a bouncy castle, where you can have good fun bouncing around."

"You should try it, Dr Laugherty," said Jack Rose.

"Do we get a chute ride in our room?" asked Penelope.

"Only the rooms with bunk beds have the chute rides, but you can book for the chute-ride game."

"OK, then. Penelope and I will both be entered for that,

please, because that sounds like fun," said Patrick.

All of the Laugherty family were very happy about this enchanted castle in deepest Dorset. Lord James Smedley-Barrington and Lady Eve Smedley-Barrington had certainly transformed the castle with all the latest gizmos and gadgets.

Jack Rose took the family into the dining room of Cough Castle, and they sat at the longest castle dining table you ever did see. It was crowded with guests.

When they finally went to bed, they all wondered what on earth the chute-ride game was all about and if the bouncy castle was like other bouncy castles they had seen and been bouncing on. They would soon find out how different it was! They all thought Cough Castle was such fun, and they wished they could stay for longer. They had forgotten about the three ghosts of the castle, but they were destined to bump into them again on the chute-ride game.

As Patrick and Penelope lay in bed, suddenly outside the castle window they heard an owl hooting. Although it was midnight, they didn't feel sleepy; they felt wide awake.

The Stonehenge Midnight Dance

When the Laugherty family had left the shop in Weymouth, Mabble Merlin took out his crystal ball and placed it on the counter. Suddenly it clouded over and became a misty-green colour. As the scene became clearer, Mabble Merlin realised he was looking at a place in Glastonbury.

Mabble Merlin loved Glastonbury. He loved the areas close by – the little towns of Frome and Shepton Mallet – and other interesting places further afield, such as Bridgwater.

The scene changed, and Mabble Merlin could see the inside of a pub. A man with thick sandy-coloured hair was standing in front of a log fire, and Mabble Merlin knew the man was thinking of buying a mirror to put above the fireplace. The man was named Seamus O'Reilly, and he was the owner of Seamus O'Reilly's Irish Bar in Glastonbury. He'd lived in Glastonbury for eight months, and he had inherited £100,000 from his grandfather, who had owned a farm in Limerick in Southern Ireland. Seamus had always wanted to live in Glastonbury, and so he'd bought the pub and spent several months renovating it to his taste. Seamus was hoping to purchase an antique mirror engraved with a Celtic design. He doubted whether he would find such a mirror, but he didn't know that Mabble Merlin was watching him through his crystal ball.

As Seamus strolled down Glastonbury High Street, Mabble Merlin's shop suddenly appeared next to a shop named Earth Spirit. On the site there had been an empty shop covered in scaffolding, but, as if by magic, the scaffolding had disappeared and Mabble Merlin's Musty Old Magical Curiosity Shop was in its place.

Seamus walked along. With his sandy hair, green eyes and unusual dress sense, he looked an interesting character. He wore a black hat, a paisley waistcoat and scarf and stripy trousers. As soon as he came to the Musty Old Magical Curiosity Shop he stopped in his tracks. He felt sure he hadn't seen the shop before, and he was intrigued, so he immediately went into the shop.

Mabble Merlin was dressed in a very similar style. He wore a tall hat with a paisley waistcoat, a lime-green scarf and striped black-and-green trousers. The lime-green scarf had four-leaf clovers printed on it.

Seamus spoke first: "Good day to you, sir," he said in a broad Irish accent.

"How are you today?" asked Mabble Merlin.

"I'm very well. I am looking for a mirror – something a bit special in a Celtic design."

"Is this what you had in mind?" asked Mabble Merlin.

He walked quickly over to a corner of the room and there, hanging on the wall, was a beautiful mirror in a frame with a Celtic pattern.

"That is exactly what I had in mind!" exclaimed Seamus.

Mabble Merlin wrapped it up in brown paper and Seamus carried it proudly back to the pub, where he hung it above the fireplace.

Seamus had a black Labrador named Guinness.

"Come and see this, Guinny," shouted Seamus. "Don't you think this is the real McCoy?"

The dog barked at the mirror, and that was strange as the dog hardly ever barked. It was normally such a soft, placid dog.

"Do you think it's haunted, Guinny, hey, boy?" Seamus asked the dog.

Then the dog suddenly fell fast asleep in front of the log fire.

As usual, that night Seamus had some local Irish musicians in the pub. Sometimes Seamus played along with the musicians, as he liked to play the bodhrán, but he decided not to play that night. His mind was on the mirror. At times he thought he could hear music coming from the mirror, and he began to think it was very strange the way he had found the very mirror he had been thinking about. And, of course, Mabble Merlin was a very strange shopkeeper. Seamus couldn't wait for the last customer to go, but at last he locked up and quickly went back to the lounge.

He looked into the mirror and he felt mesmerised. It looked as if the mirror was made of liquid silver. He bent over and prodded the mirror with his finger. The glass seems to be quivering, and suddenly, without warning, Seamus was sucked into the mirror. There was a popping sound, like a champagne cork being pulled out of a bottle, and then Seamus was falling downwards.

He stopped falling, and, as if by pure magic, he found himself at Stonehenge, on Salisbury Plain.

He looked around him at the green rolling hills of the English countryside in the distance, and directly in front of him were the huge Stonehenge standing stones. He'd always wanted to go to Stonehenge, and it felt like a dream come true. In fact, he thought it was a dream. Coming from Limerick in Ireland, he had learnt to expect the unexpected, and so he was open to the strange and unusual.

Up until now he hadn't had the time to go to Stonehenge; he'd been working so hard renovating the pub. But now here he was, so he made up his mind to enjoy the moment.

"It must be a magical mirror," he said out loud. "No matter! No worries!"

He put his hand on one of the huge stones, and the stone

lit up with a bright lilac glow. Another stone turned bright orange when he touched it, and another turned a bright yellow. He felt a tingle of energy up his spine.

He said out loud, "I've got the power."

Suddenly a voice boomed out, "Welcome to the Stonehenge Midnight Dance."

Then in the middle of Stonehenge a group of little people popped up from out of the ground and they began to play their musical instruments.

Seamus thought they looked like leprechauns – the little people of Limerick. One of them played the fiddle, one played the Irish flute, one had a banjo and one played the bodhrán. Then the craziest thing of all happened. Seamus suddenly felt as if he could dance. He'd always wanted to be able to dance really well, and suddenly he could. He danced to Irish jig music, weaving in and out of the standing stones. He weaved this way, then that way, in and out, faster and faster and faster and faster until he became a blur and he thought he might meet himself coming back. He was thrilled and enchanted by the power of the dance, with the Irish music playing loudly in his ears and the standing stones flashing different colours.

Suddenly he began to slow down, and then the music changed. He danced into the centre of the standing stones, jumping up into the air, kicking his legs and doing somersaults and cartwheels. He didn't want to stop, but eventually the music slowed down and came to a complete stop. As if he was a famous dancer on a stage, he took a bow.

Now, for the first time, he noticed he was wearing green velvet trousers and a green velvet jacket and a lime-green scarf patterned with four-leaf clovers. He was also wearing a green velvet trilby, and green shoes decorated with gold four-leaf clovers and a huge gold buckle.

The musicians were only two feet tall – or maybe three feet at the most. They ran over to shake hands and to hug and kiss him as if he was the star of the show. They were just like the little people of Limerick; he'd always been told about them making dreams come true.

They did look a bit peculiar. One had a flat, round face with great big eyes, huge eyelashes and hair stuck up on end. This strange-looking creature was female, and she played the tambourine and the maraccas. Another one had a face like a crumpled prune, with huge purple eyes and lilac hair. This one was male, and he played the violin. Another one looked like a cute hedgehog, with little eyes like pieces of coal, a hedgehog nose and sky-blue hair stuck out in all directions, like a loo brush. She played the bodhrán. Another of the musicians had the look of a typical leprechaun. He had big bulging eyes, a pot belly and black straw-like hair. He played the banjo. Another had a face like a squashed tomato. She had pink hair, and she wore ruby-red lipstick. She played the Irish fiddle. They were stranger than any people Seamus had ever heard of, that's for sure.

They all said, "Thank you, Seamus," and then he suddenly felt himself falling.

When he stopped falling, he was back in his pub in Glastonbury, standing in front of the antique mirror. His Labrador was still asleep.

He looked at the clock – it was 1 a.m. – and he remembered that it was midnight when he first looked in the mirror.

He just thought, 'Wow! That was a very strange experience.'

He decided to go upstairs to bed, because he felt so sleepy after all that dancing. He knew he would never ever forget his magical experience of the Stonehenge Midnight Dance.

As he climbed the stairs to bed, he was humming the tune of the Irish jig music, and he looked forward to playing the same Irish jig music with the local Irish musicians when they came back to the pub.

In the Closet

When the Laugherty family arrived home from Dorset, they told Miles about Cough Castle. They told him about the chute and that they had played a game in the middle of the night where the castle was under siege. They had ridden in little bunk beds through secret passageways and underground caverns until they had come to a bouncy castle. By means of antigravity they had floated above the floor in a large room where everything was made out of a soft foam material that looked exactly like wood. Castle guests seemed to be dancing in the centre of the floor, but they were only holographic images and it was possible to float right through them.

Miles listened intently.

"That sounds so exciting," he said when they finished, "but it doesn't sound like you got any sleep."

"And the castle is haunted by three ghosts," piped up Oliver.

"And — don't tell me," said Miles: "you saw them all."

"We all saw the knight and the cook, but only I saw the young girl, Ella, carrying her rag doll!" Daisy exclaimed excitedly.

"Well, it was very different from a camping holiday in Wales," said Patrick. "I rather enjoyed the chute game. It was a bit like Disneyland inside a real castle."

"The upstairs rooms had glass floors, with little bunk beds in alcoves, and the beds could move about at the flick of a switch," said Oliver.

"It sounds more like Fantasy Land than Disneyland," said Miles, handing round cups of tea.

They talked for thirty minutes without pausing for breath, before they finally all sat down on the sofa in the living room and had a cup of tea and biscuits. Miles was glad to have the family back.

After a while Miles went into the kitchen to make more tea. He noticed that Milly was still not showing the correct time. He took the tea on a silver tray into the living room, where the tired family were sitting. Then Patrick unwrapped the French kitchen clock, Claudette de Seconds, and Penelope unwrapped her Egyptian jewellery.

Patrick asked Miles to take Milly off the wall and put the new clock in her place.

Miles immediately went into the kitchen and put Milly on the shelf in the closet in the hall. When he put Claudette de Seconds on the wall, the kitchen immediately felt very regal, like a French court. Everyone had to sit up straight and had to speak properly – or it felt a bit like they had to.

Poor Milly sat on the dusty shelf in the closet. She couldn't help it, but she started to sob.

"Oh dear, oh dear, oh dear!" she kept saying.

Then suddenly she nearly jumped off the shelf with shock when she heard a voice pipe up: "Oh, heavens! What is the matter with you?"

The voice was coming from something wrapped up in gift paper sitting on the shelf below her.

"I'm London Melody. I'm a new picture clock. I was purchased recently, but I am sure my new owners have forgotten about me."

"Oh, hello, London Melody. I'm pleased to meet you. I know it's so silly, but I'm very sentimental and someone new has arrived: Claudette de Seconds has taken my place."

Milly started to cry again, and in a moment she was sobbing her heart out, unable to speak.

"Come on, Milly – don't be so silly," whispered London Melody. "There must be something we can do to help you."

"Well, Mog Og would help if he knew I was in here, but the door is closed and he can't hear me. I expect he is sleeping as usual."

"Oh dear!" exclaimed London Melody in her posh London accent. "He doesn't sound much help, does he? Do you know anyone with special powers?" asked London Melody.

"Well, there is one clock, Polly Quazar, who is telepathic. She may be able to get a message to Mog Og."

"Well, then," said London Melody, "let's get a telepathic message to Polly Quazar. As a matter of fact, I want to get out of this dusty cupboard too. I ought to be put on a wall, where I can be admired by the family. I'm supposed to be a birthday present. I've been getting rather fed up in this cupboard with no one to talk to."

"Well, you have me now," said Milly forlornly.

"I hope Mog Og can help and that I go and do what I'm supposed to do instead of hiding away in this cupboard."

"Oh, you're so funny!" exclaimed Milly.

She was feeling so much better having London Melody to talk to.

"Oh, I feel so hemmed in," cried London Melody, "wrapped up in this silly wrapping paper! Right then, Milly – let's get a telepathic message to Polly Quazar to tell Mog Og to come to the rescue.

Then London Melody concentrated her mind and spoke telepathically to Polly Quazar. She asked Polly Quazar to send a telepathic message to Mog Og.

Mog Og was sitting under the apple tree in the garden when he telepathically heard his name being called. He knew it was Polly Quazar, and he rushed into the house and into the dining room.

"Hey, Polly, what's up?" asked Mog Og, feeling a bit worried.

"Oh, Mog Og, Milly is in the closet on a dusty shelf and there's a new picture clock, London Melody, on the bottom shelf wrapped in paper."

"Goodness me!" exclaimed Mog Og, scratching his head. "That's a very strange situation, but I'll go to the rescue. Tell them both not to worry – Mog Og is coming."

Polly Quazar sent the message telepathically to London Melody, who informed Milly that Mog Og would help.

Later that night Mog Og opened the closet door and went in to talk to Milly and London Melody.

"Oh, Mog Og!" cried Milly.

She was over the moon to see the fat cat, who was laden with armfuls of handkerchiefs. He handed one of them to Milly.

Milly started to cry again as she told Mog Og about Claudette de Seconds taking her place. Milly's mascara was running down her clock face, and her pink lipstick was smudged. Mog Og wiped a tear away from her blue eyes.

"I will help you if I can. Of course I will help you, silly! Cats always help – you know that. You trust me, don't you? Never mind that silly French court clock, Claudette de Seconds. She should still be at a French court – or in France, at least. She's a long way from home, and she might start crying when she gets homesick. She won't have the kind of life she's used to – having servants, and having her powder put on her face for her, and even having her hair brushed. I wouldn't be surprised if she even had someone to brush her teeth. She probably didn't do anything for herself, so she might start asking us to run around after her. You, Milly, powder your own nose, put your own perfume on and paint your face all by yourself. I don't expect Claudette will want to do the same."

Suddenly London Melody piped up: "Mog Og, would you be able to help me get this silly wrapping paper off me?"

"Well," said Mog Og, "the best thing to do is to get Penelope to find you. After all, you are a birthday present. What I suggest is that I carry you into the living room so Penelope can find you."

"That's an excellent idea, Mog Og. I'm so pleased to meet you."

"And I'm pleased to meet you. I suspect you look spectacular without wrapping paper on," said Mog Og.

"I assure you, you won't be disappointed. I am a picture clock, so I am tailor-made to be admired. I can change my picture, and I have lots of other talents to. I want to get cracking, and to be on show – not sitting on a musty shelf that smells of old shoes."

"I think it is old shoes that are causing the smell," said Mog Og. "I've got my best eau de cologne on; I have to smell good as I've got a busy social life."

London Melody started to laugh, and the others joined in – even Milly.

"Listen, Milly – you keep smiling. I'll be back when I've thought of something," said Mog Og.

"OK, Mog Og," said Milly and London Melody.

"We'll both wait. We'll be patient," said London Melody.

Mog Og left the dusty closet, and he walked up and down the hallway until he was dizzy. By then it was nearly midnight – the time when cats can think best. He suddenly had a brainwave, and a moment later he tapped on the closet door.

"OK, Milly, I have a cunning plan: I am going to have a walk tonight and see what I can find. I feel a journey is in order."

London Melody piped up: "Wherever you go, will you take me? It ought to be better than sitting on this dusty bottom shelf."

"Of course, London Melody, you can come with me."

Mog Og's Late-Night Journey

Late that night Mog Og crept out through the cat flap. He jumped on to the dustbin and over the high garden wall. Then he made his way over rooftops, garden fences and walls, and down very dark alleys. At one point he was chased by some loud alley cats with fleas. Finally he crossed a bridge and ended up in the Hyde Park area, where, in a familiar cobbled street, he came to a shop, and he was so pleased to see that the lights were on.

'Excellent!' he thought. 'This could be the breakthrough for Milly Dilly Dally.'

He liked to call her that because she did dilly-dally an awful lot.

He was a straight-talking cat with a lot of ambition — albeit a fat cat that loved sleeping. 'But hey," he thought, 'who doesn't love sleeping?' But tonight Mog Og was too busy to sleep.

"Mog Og's on a mission," he shouted.

At that moment a female cat turned the corner. Her fur was milky satin cream and she had an elegant walk. He was enraptured.

As she walked past she whispered in a soft velvet feminine voice, "I'm Mystique, but you can call me Mysty."

"I certainly will!" said Mog Og. "And I'm Mog Og, but you can call me Mog or Og."

"I'll call you Mog, if I may," said Mysty. "Where are you off to so late at night?"

"It's a long, long story, Mysty, but I'm going to that shop over the road and I'd be really happy if you could join me on the mission. I think you'll enjoy it, Mysty," said Mog Og confidently.

"OK," said Mysty, sounding like a jazz singer with a smoky velvet voice.

Then they both rushed over the road to the Musty Old Magical Curiosity Shop, which was in between a pub named The Cat's Whiskers and a very large hotel named The Cumbersome Hotel. Mog Og and Mysty went into the shop through a cat flap in the door, and there in the shop was the old shopkeeper with his owl on his shoulder. The owl had the largest, oddest, wide-open brown eyes. He was wearing a monocle. He was a white owl.

In an armchair in the shop was a Persian cat with fluffy fur and amber-yellow eyes. They twinkled with humour. The cat was named Twilight, and it was stuck between two worlds.

"Well, well, well, well," said Twilight, "look what the cat's dragged in! Two cats for the price of one."

The owl hooted with laughter, and his monocle fell off his face. Then he coughed and cleared his throat and became serious.

"How can I help, cos I am the owl of all knowing."

He blinked, and his brown eyes twinkled.

The shopkeeper looked at the owl and said, "This owl is the owl of wisdom; if you want to know what to do, he'll have the answer for you."

"Well, it's like this," said Mog Og: "I have a friend, Milly Paris. She's a kitchen clock. She's broken her hands, or rather they're stuck fast – and, besides that, she can't tell the time very well. I would like to know what we can do, Mr Owl."

The owl cleared his throat and began to speak: "I believe", said the owl, "she must go to Tick-Tock School at once and learn to tell the time. Her hands need greasing with goose fat and tickling with a goose feather. They will do that for her at the school, and they'll also help her with her times tables and teach her to tick-tock perfectly. OK?" said the owl.

The owl seemed very professional and knowledgeable. He spoke just like doctor.

"Yes. Wow!" said Mog Og. "That sounds like a plan! It sounds excellent, fantastic, fabulous, incredible," said Mog Og.

"The only problem is," asked Mysty, "where is Tick-Tock School?"

"You see that door on your left – it says 'Private' – well, that is the entrance to our Tick-Tock School. It's a private school for clocks, you see."

"OK, that's just grand," said Mysty.

Mysty was an Irish cat. She'd left Ireland as a stowaway cat on a small coble – she wanted to see the world.

"Well, Mog," said Mysty, "I think we ought to go and get Milly. I expect she has been crying herself to sleep."

"Yes," said the owl, "the sooner, the better. You bring her here and we'll set to work on her. I'm sure she'll learn quickly – most of them do, you see. In fact, we don't have any failures, only successes. And if there is anything else she wants to learn, we'll help her with that too. We also run a clock hospital. We have specialists in heartbeats, psychotherapists, psychologists, hypnotherapists, dieticians and make-up artists. Basically we have the best in health care. We also do face improvements, including facelifts – anything to lighten the burden! There is a beauty salon with nail technicians and massage therapists. We also have a beautician for cats."

"Oh," said Mysty, "what can you do for me?"

The owl piped up: "I said *beautician* not *magician*," and he laughed until his monocle fell out of his wise brown eye.

"Oh, I could do with a manicure," said Mysty. "My nails are really sharp."

"Oh," said the owl. "And what else would you like?"

"I'd like longer whiskers and painted nails – a Mayan heart symbol on one, a diamond on another."

"Oh, yes," said the owl, "like the symbols on playing cards."

"And I'd like some new perfume," said Mysty.

Mog Og decided that this cat was 'high maintenance', but the owl was keeping up with all her needs and wants.

"Oh," said the owl, "we have some new perfume: Cat Magick No. 5."

"Sounds cool!" said Mog Og. "What have you got in the way of aftershave for me?"

"We've got a new fragrance: Cool Cat No. 7 eau de cologne. I will get you everything you need," said the wise owl, and he laughed until his mortar-board hat fell off.

"Right then," said the old shopkeeper, "I think we're ready to rock and roll."

"You rock and I'll roll," said the owl, laughing again until his head nearly fell off.

Mabble Merlin clapped his hands in delight. There was a quick burst of lightning and the cats' hairs stood up on end.

"Wow! What was that?" said Mog Og.

"Lightning never strikes twice," said the owl. "So run, cats, run cos there could be a downpour," said the owl.

So off Mog Og and Mysty ran, all the way home, over ditches and benches and fences and through hedges and up lanes and down lanes and over fields, past cows, pigs and owls.

Finally they reached home, out of breath. They crept into the hallway and saw that Milly and London Melody were fast asleep.

Welcome to Tick-Tock School

"Milly, Milly, wake up, wake up. We've found a private school just for you, where you can learn to tick-tock. They will teach you your times tables and how to tell the time – and anything else you need to learn. We're going to sneak you out of the house."

Then London Melody woke up. She wanted to go with them, just for the journey and the fun of it.

"Can I come, Mog Og, please?" she asked.

"Of course you can, London Melody. When we have caught our breath we're going to run like the wind to the Musty Old Magical Curiosity Shop. If you like, you can stay for a while and do the tick-tock course. You can also learn other things, such as dancing, if you want to. Or you can make your own perfume. Why not call it Love at First Sight? Wow! I bet you'll be famous with that perfume. Come on, Milly – quietly does it!" said Mog Og.

Milly couldn't believe her luck. She was so excited. Mog Og helped her and London Melody down off the shelf, and the two clocks suddenly sprouted little legs to help them to be able to run, run, run, through hedges and over bridges and ditches – basically to run as fast as the wind in a midnight storm.

The two cats and the two clocks sneaked out of the cat flap and hurried down back lanes and through hedges, under bridges and over bridges. They almost flew over the moon in their haste. Past cows and pigs and hens and ducks and geese they ran, until at last they reached the Musty Old Magical Curiosity Shop out of breath.

The four of them stood in front of the old shopkeeper and the owl.

"Now, who have we here?" said the owl.

"Well, this is Milly Paris and this is London Melody."

"Why are you wrapped up in wrapping paper, London Melody? Do you not want to take that off? All you have to do is think that it's been taken off and it will be done," said Mabble Merlin. "In fact, as I was the one that wrapped you I say let it be undone."

Mabble Merlin clapped his hands and London Melody could then be seen and the wrapping paper was gone.

Mog Og, Mysty and Milly thought London Melody was such a pretty, realistic picture of London. The picture was of the city at night-time, and it showed several double-decker buses moving over Westminster Bridge with Big Ben in the background. There was a large moon and little twinkling stars.

London Melody enjoyed the admiring glances everyone gave her. She was so glad the wrapping paper was off and that she could at last breathe. She had felt suffocated in the deep-blue wrapping paper.

"Well," said Mabble Merlin, "you certainly haven't wasted any time in getting Milly here, have you, Mog Og?"

Mabble Merlin was wearing a purple pointed hat and a purple cloak, and on the cloak were strange symbols and equations from the works of great mathematicians and scientists, like Pythagoras and Einstein. Inside the cloak was the equation $E = mc^2$. Magical numbers swirled inside his hat, bouncing up and down like numbered balls in a lottery machine. These numbers were alive – they could tell the truth and they could solve equations.

Milly's eyes were wide with wonder, and so were Mog Og's and Mysty's and London Melody's. Of course, the owl's eyes were always wide with wonder, and so were Twilight's.

"Don't worry," said the owl. "We'll get you straightened out, Milly."

The owl went over to Milly.

"Any back problems?" he asked.

The owl was also a doctor, and he dutifully took out a stethoscope and listened to Milly's heartbeat. She had been worrying a lot lately – especially since she had been put on the dusty shelf in the closet.

"Oh dear, Milly! You have a few beats missing and your chest is wheezing. I'll give you a spoonful of cough medicine for that, and a mixture of heather honey, sunflower honey and lavender honey. If you take this medicine, your chest will be perfect. Honey is really good for your voice too," said Dr Hoot-Hoot. "You will be OK. After a four-month stay here with us, you'll be fine," said Dr Hoot-Hoot.

"A four-month stay!" exclaimed Milly, almost fainting.

Her little legs had turned to jelly.

"Well, actually, it will only be four days, because we'll speed up time with a bit of hocus-pocus. We'll do a bit of time-slipping or time-bending," said Dr Hoot-Hoot.

"Oh dear!" said Milly. "I do hope it is only four days."

"Leave it to me," said Dr Hoot-Hoot. "Mabble Merlin always has to speed up time in the school, because no one likes months and months going by, that's for sure, when they can get away with a few days. This place, as you know, is no ordinary place – it's no ordinary shop."

"You can say that again!" said Milly.

"I agree," said Mog Og.

"So do I," said Mysty.

"And I do too," piped up London Melody.

"Only if you're lucky enough, will you see the shop," said Dr Hoot-Hoot. "We can be invisible if we want to be, and we can disappear in a puff of smoke. We're not always in the same place. We move about like gypsies. A rolling stone gathers no moss. We like to keep our customers guessing."

"Well, that's fascinating," said Mog Og. "I guess we are lucky, lucky, lucky!"

Suddenly Lucky, the magical cat, appeared. With her long curly whiskers, big green eyes and black midnight fur she did look very strange.

"Did someone call my name?" she asked.

"Oh, I'm pleased to meet you," said Mog Og.

"Just call me Lucky."

Then Mog Og felt so lucky that he wanted to dance and sing. There was an old dusty piano in the room, and Mog Og went to the piano and started to play and sing. The others all felt very happy, and they started to sing along. Suddenly, as if by magic, musical instruments appeared. The sometimes-invisible cat, Lucky, played the flute, Twilight played the fiddle and Dr Hoot-Hoot played the double bass. Milly started to sing; London Melody joined in in a beautiful angelic voice, and Mysty joined in too. She sang like a jazz singer, with a smooth, soulful voice.

As if by magic, the shop turned into a jazz saloon. Mabble Merlin started to dance. Musical notes with rhythm and a bass beat appeared from his hands, and musical stardust appeared in the air.

His clothes had changed. He was now wearing a white suit with a white trilby. He looked like a 1920s jazz-club singer. He wore braces and a multicoloured striped shirt.

"Let the real music begin. Let the real dance begin," he said, and he clapped his hands.

Suddenly a 1920s dancer appeared – a flapper girl. It was Zelda Fitzgerald. She and Mabble Merlin danced the jitterbug, the charleston and the cha-cha.

They all had really enjoyed the evening. Milly felt she was in good hands. When the dancing finally ended, it was time for Mog Og, London Melody and Mystique to go home, but it was pouring down outside.

"Look at the weather," said Mog Og. "It never rains – it just pours."

"Don't worry," said Dr Hoot-Hoot. "I've got something for each of you so you won't get wet on your travels.

Dr Hoot-Hoot gave Mog Og a little tartan jacket. It was waterproof and it was just what Mog Og wanted. He loved tartan. Then Dr Hoot-Hoot gave Mysty a large umbrella, and he wrapped London Melody in deep-pink waterproof wrapping paper tied with a crimson bow. On the wrapping paper he put a gift tag: 'To Penelope from Miles, with love from the Musty Old Magical Curiosity Shop. Happy birthday'.

The friends waved goodbye to Milly, Mabble Merlin, Twilight, Dr Hoot-Hoot and Lucky.

Mog Og's tartan jacket was a magical jacket. It made his fur change colour from grey to a mixture of black, ginger, white and tortoiseshell.

London Melody Goes on Show

Mysty said goodnight to Mog Og reluctantly. She didn't have far to go to get home – she lived round the corner from the Musty Old Magical Curiosity Shop – in the cobbled street known as Kensington Cobbles.

Mog Og said to Mysty he would meet her again in a few days' time at the same place. They stood staring at each other. He was just going to give her a goodnight kiss when there was a big flash of lightning and they almost jumped out of their skins.

Then Mysty ran helter-skelter back to her home, while Mog Og and London Melody ran like the wind back to their home in Bayswater. London Melody looked hilarious running along next to Mog Og in her bright-pink shiny wrapping paper and crimson bow. She was still singing, and Mog Og in his tartan jacket was also singing, even though they were both running as fast as they could go. They ran over fields, over hills, under hills, up trees, down trees, over hedges, under hedges, over cows, over pigs, over geese, overground, underground, over barn owls and over barnyards, over turkeys and chickens and sheep, over the moon and over the stars, and finally they arrived home – home, sweet home.

They crept in through the cat flap. It was a bit of a squash for London Melody, but somehow she just managed it. She decided she wasn't going back on the dusty shelf – she was going to lie on the sofa and go to sleep. She'd had an eventful night! Mog Og, of course, lay on the fluffy mat in front of the fire. Before long they had both fallen fast asleep.

The next morning, Miles got up very early as he always did. He went into the living room to open the curtains, and he was immediately struck by the sight of a large present on the settee. He realised that it must be the picture clock that Patrick had bought for Penelope's birthday, but he couldn't understand how on earth it came to be in pink wrapping paper. He was sure that, when Mabble Merlin had delivered it, it had been in deep-blue wrapping paper. He guessed that the wrapping paper had been damaged, and that was why it had been replaced. He decided to give Penelope the birthday present straight away because he wanted to know if it was indeed the picture clock.

At that moment Penelope appeared, and Miles gave her the present (because the little gift tag now read – 'To Penelope from Miles').

"Oh, that's so kind of you, Miles," she said.

Penelope opened the present and saw London Melody for the first time.

"It's so beautiful, Miles. It's so unusual. You just can't stop looking at it, can you?"

'I hope you can't stop looking at me,' thought London Melody. 'I am so glad to be on display instead of wrapped up in bright paper, and feeling suffocated.'

"I'll put it on the wall for you, Penelope," said Miles. "I've got another small present for your birthday, but I'll give you that at the party on the actual day."

"Oh, that's very sweet of you, Miles."

Penelope looked at the picture clock again. It was mesmerising. Then she noticed the words on the bottom of the picture, which read, 'The Possibilities Are Endless – London Melody'.

There was a tear in Penelope's eye as she read the words – they were so sentimental and profound, and she felt that the possibilities were indeed endless.

When Mog Og finally woke up, still in his tartan jacket, he looked up to see London Melody smiling sweetly at him. Now her scene showed a beautiful autumn day in London, with the leaves falling from the trees. It looked like Hyde Park. Mog Og thought for a moment that he could see Mysty walking in and out of the trees.

The Invisibility Mirror

After the events of the night before, Mabble Merlin was just sitting having a cup of tea; he was wondering how his customers were doing. Mabble Merlin liked to ensure that all his customers were happy and contented – and even enchanted. He liked to know that when a customer bought something from his shop he or she would enjoy its magic. He maintained an interest in their lives.

Sometimes a customer purchased something and hadn't a clue that it had any hidden powers.

Mabble Merlin's crystal ball, which was hidden in a secret compartment of the shop counter when not in use, was now on the counter. Suddenly he noticed that the crystal ball was clouding over, which meant there was a vision coming through.

Gradually the cloudiness disappeared and a very clear scene appeared. Mabble Merlin found himself looking at a scene in the Lion and Unicorn Inn in Pluckley, where Sally and Richard Knight were standing in front of the antique mirror they had recently bought. They were in love and happy, and they looked at each other in the mirror, thinking how happy they were to have bought the pub and to be together.

Suddenly they felt a very strong tug – just as if an invisible hand had come out of the mirror and was pulling them into it.

When the feeling stopped, they both looked at each other, and Richard said, "Oh, boy, what was that?"

Sally said, "Did you have a strange feeling of being pulled into the mirror?"

Richard replied, "I felt the same thing."

Mabble Merlin watched the scene in the crystal ball, engrossed in it.

Sally and Richard went downstairs, where the chef, Joseph Grylls, was in the kitchen, cooking breakfast for the guests.

Sally and Richard went in, as they did every morning, and said, "Hi, Joe."

Joe didn't look up. He continued cooking, and he seemed to be ignoring them.

Richard went straight up to Joe and patted him on the back, and the chef screamed, "What the heck was that! Oh, dear Lord! This place is haunted."

Sally said, "Stop kidding around, Joseph Grylls."

When Joseph still didn't look up from cooking the breakfast, they realised they were invisible. Something really strange had happened to them and they both realised that it was connected in some way with the mirror.

"Come on," said Richard. "That antique mirror has magic powers – it has made us invisible. It must have happened when we felt that strange tugging sensation."

They both scrambled upstairs as fast as their legs could carry them, and once again they looked intently into the mirror. After a few minutes they both felt a tug on their bodies, as though by an invisible hand, and they guessed that they probably weren't invisible any more.

"Come on," said Richard, "let's check this out."

They both scrambled downstairs once again and dashed into the kitchen as fast as their legs could carry them.

They both said, "Hi, Joe."

"Morning, Sally. Morning, Richard," replied Joe. "Are you both OK? You both look as if you have seen a ghost."

"We're fine, Joe," said Richard, and they both gave Joe a big hug.

"Hey, steady on, guys! Is it my birthday?" he said, and they all laughed.

"Well, if you two haven't seen a ghost, I certainly have felt one. This place is haunted. A few minutes ago someone patted me on the shoulder and I thought it was you, Richard, but oh boy! There was no one there. It's a wonder I've managed to cook breakfast," said Joe.

"Well, it looks lovely, as it always does, Joe," said Richard.

Sally and Richard went upstairs again, and Sally said, "You know what, Richard: I think we could have fun with this magic mirror. Just for one day we'll play a few pranks on the guests. They have been looking a bit tired and in need of a pick-me-up — we'll make their hair stand on end if it isn't already."

Sally and Richard knew exactly what to do. They went to the mirror and stared at each other in the glass. They were scared and yet excited, and they felt compelled to become invisible again. They stared intently at each other in the mirror, and then suddenly they felt the strange tug as if an invisible hand had come out of the mirror. Suddenly it stopped, and it felt as though time had stood still. They felt the same — they could still see each other and they could see the room just as it always had been, but they knew that other people wouldn't be able to see them. They dashed downstairs as fast as their legs could carry them.

Malcolm Drury was staying at the inn in order to visit relatives, who lived nearby, before the hectic Christmas season. He owned a turkey farm in Norfolk.

Malcolm was looking forward to a well-earned breakfast. He went over to the breakfast buffet, which looked delicious, and he piled up his plate with pork sausages, bacon, two fried eggs, black pudding, tomatoes, mushrooms and hash browns. He took the huge breakfast to his table. It was so heavy he could hardly carry it. He

put it on the place mat on the table and went back to the breakfast buffet to pour himself some tea and a glass of orange juice, and while he was there he popped some bread in the toaster. As he waited for the toast to pop up, he was humming a tune.

Whilst his back was turned, Sally and Richard arrived in the dining room. Sally ate the mushrooms and tomatoes and Richard ate the sausages and black pudding.

When Malcolm got back to the table with his cup of tea, orange juice and toast and finally sat down, he noticed that the black pudding and sausages weren't on the plate, and neither were the mushrooms or tomatoes. He thought another guest had taken the food, or maybe a dog had stolen it – either that or he was getting rather forgetful in his old age.

He decided to go and get some more food. He replenished the plate with three pork sausages and two pieces of black pudding, mushrooms and tomatoes; but whilst he was piling up the plate Sally drank Malcolm's orange juice and Richard drank his tea.

When Malcolm got back to his seat, he didn't at first notice that the tea and the orange juice had been drunk; he was too busy tucking into his black pudding and pork sausages. At last he picked up his cup of tea and saw that the cup was empty.

"What on earth is going on?" he shouted in a really loud, gruff voice.

The waitress came out of the kitchen and asked, "Is everything OK, Mr Drury?"

"Have you got a dog in this place, stealing my food and drinking my tea?"

"There's no dogs in here, Mr Drury."

"Don't worry. I'll pour myself another cup of tea and another glass of orange juice," said Mr Drury in a very gruff voice.

Meanwhile Sally had stuck the toast to the back of Mr Drury's jumper, and when he walked away to get another cup of tea and a glass of orange juice the waitress saw the toast hanging there. She thought it looked very funny, but she knew that he'd go mad when he realised the toast had disappeared as well. She didn't want him shouting in his gruff voice any more, so she realised she would somehow have to get the toast off the back of his jumper. She decided to keep talking to Mr Drury to distract him.

"How are you enjoying your holiday, Mr Drury?"

"To be honest, I've really enjoyed it here. It's clean and friendly, and Sally and Richard are two of the nicest people you could ever meet. But I do think you must have a phantom dog. I've heard stories about phantom dogs in Norfolk, and I believe they exist."

The waitress of the inn, Beth Appleby, had heard that the ghost of a little dog was sometimes seen in the village of Pluckley. She thought it was best to agree that a phantom dog must have drunk Mr Drury's tea and orange juice.

Sally and Richard thought it was great doing the prank on Malcolm; but when they heard him say that he was really enjoying his stay, and that Sally and Richard were lovely people, they felt a bit guilty. So they dashed upstairs as fast as their legs could carry them and stared into the mirror to quickly reverse the process.

When they were no longer invisible, they raced downstairs and into the dining room, where Mr Drury was just finishing his breakfast and Beth had somehow managed to get the toast off the back of his jumper and on to his plate.

"How good to see you both!" exclaimed Malcolm as they walked calmly into the room.

"You too," said Richard. "We were thinking, Malcolm, that we would like to buy your turkeys this year for our restaurant – we know you look after your turkeys very well."

"Indeed I do, and you look after me very well in your lovely restaurant," said Malcolm, "apart from the phantom dog you've got."

"Sorry about that," said Richard apologetically.

They all laughed together, and every time Sally thought about the toast clinging to Mr Drury's jumper she laughed a little bit more, but they still felt guilty about playing pranks on him. He was a lovely man, so they thought they would buy his turkeys – that was sure to cheer him up, as they would have a lot of people in their restaurant over Christmas for turkey dinners. They would require a lot of turkeys, so it could make a good sale for him.

Needless to say, he was very happy about the deal. He

asked them if they wanted the cranberry sauce that his wife, Marjorie, made at their Norfolk farm, so Sally and Richard also bought their cranberry sauce and their free-range eggs and their organic honey and their royal jelly.

Mabble Merlin had watched the whole episode in the crystal ball, and he was very pleased indeed that Malcolm Drury had got to sell the produce from his Norfolk farm to Sally and Richard Knight. He did think the pranks were very funny, but they were also a little bit mean, so he was so pleased with Sally and Richard for making amends by deciding to buy Malcolm Drury's farm produce.

A Ride on the Carousel

One morning the school teacher, Miss Carol Sums, went into school early, and she saw that the clock on the wall was covered with orange paint, with flour and with egg yolk. It was certainly no joke for the school clock, Erica English, and Miss Sums thought she would try to wash the clock face with soapy water.

She put the clock on the draining board and filled the sink with soapy water.

At nine o'clock all the pupils were in class, and Miss Sums asked them who was responsible for the state of the clock.

"Come on, pupils – someone must have done it," she said.

Three hands went up.

"So tell me exactly what the three of you have done to this poor clock," Miss Sums demanded.

Callum Chuckle said he was very, very, very sorry, but he'd thrown an egg at the clock.

"I'm very, very sorry, Miss Sums."

The little tyke started to cry for fear he might get put in the naughty corner.

"Don't worry, I won't put you in the naughty corner. Instead you can help wash the face of the clock," said Miss Sums.

Another little tyke, Natalie Apple, owned up that she had thrown flour at the clock when she was making fairy cakes.

"I didn't mean to, Miss Sums. I'm very sorry."

"OK, Natalie. Don't worry. Mistakes happen," said Miss Sums.

The last little tyke, Jason Jaffa, said that he'd put the paint on the face of the clock by mistake.

"I'm very sorry, Miss Sums. I didn't mean to throw the orange paint."

"All your apologies are accepted," said Miss Sums.

Later on in the busy day, Miss Sums went over to the sink and picked up the clock on the draining board, but she accidentally dropped the clock back into the soapy water in the sink.

"Oh, dear! Oh, dear me! How can I be so silly?"

Miss Sums took the clock out of the soapy water. The clock just wouldn't work. The soapy water had got into the lungs of the clock and Erica couldn't breathe. She couldn't tick and tock. Miss Sums felt awful.

Erica had soapy water in her eyes and in her nose and in her mouth and in her hair. The paint and flour and egg yolk was no longer on her face, but now she had another problem: the water had got into her body. She felt dreadful.

Miss Sums didn't know what to do. She only knew she needed help from somewhere. She said a little prayer to herself, and then suddenly she turned around and one of the pupils, Tamsin Sunshine, was handing her a little card she had found inside one of the library books. It was a business card, and it read, 'Clocks repaired for free at the Musty Old Magical Curiosity Shop, 35 Peek-a-Boo Street, Scarborough'.

Miss Sums immediately decided to take the clock to the shop, and she decided to take the three little tykes with her.

They eventually found the shop in the centre of Scarborough, between a bakery named Dainty Cakes and a fish-and-chip shop named Cod Plaice. Their school was in Osmotherley in the Yorkshire Dales, so it was a nice day out for the children to go to Scarborough.

Natalie Apple's parents were farmers; they owned Apple Farm in Osmotherley. There was a campsite on part of their land, and this campsite wasn't far from a sheep dip, where the sheep got put into disinfected water before they got their fleeces sheared.

Osmotherley is a beautiful little quaint English village.

Miss Sums went into the quaint old shop, and the little old doorbell rang as the door opened. Mabble Merlin stood in the middle of the shop.

"Well, hello, children."

"Hello, Mr Shopkeeper," said the children all at the same time.

"How can I help you all today?"

He went over to the shop counter and there was suddenly a tray full of toffee apples. Mabble Merlin gave each of the children a toffee apple, and he handed Miss Sums a paper bag with sweets in it to give to the rest of the children in the class when she got back to the school.

"How can I help you today?" he asked again.

Miss Sums handed the clock to Mabble Merlin.

"Oh, I see. It looks as though it's been in soapy water."

"Yes – exactly! That was my mistake. I dropped it into a sink filled with soapy water."

"Accidents do happen."

Suddenly the owl sitting in the window piped up: "And naughty children do naughty things!"

The children turned round and the owl started to laugh, which made the children laugh. Even Miss Sums started to laugh.

"Well," said the owl, "it looks as though you need a ride on the carousel. Make your way through the archway, and take your places on the carousel."

They all walked through the archway, and there in front of them was a very large carousel with gleaming white horses, and they all got on to their own gleaming white horse. The carousel turned round and round, and up and down went the horses, way up into the air. When it eventually came to a full stop, they saw that they were at a fairground.

They wasted no time. All of them ran over to the ghost train and climbed aboard. They all screamed when the spiders touched their hair.

After the ghost train, they went on the one-armed bandits and they won lots of money; they also went on 'hook a duck', and Miss Sums won so many stuffed toys that she had enough for all the children in her class. After that, they went on the helter-skelter, and after that they all had some candyfloss from the candyfloss stall. Even Miss Sums had candyfloss. They had never had rainbow-coloured candyfloss before.

They then went inside the Hall of Crazy Mirrors, where the mirrors made them look small, tall, fat and thin. It was hilarious, and they laughed so much!

Suddenly Jason Jaffa piped up: "Miss Sums, Miss Sums, we haven't won a goldfish."

At that moment a sideshow appeared, and a clown asked them if they wanted to win a goldfish. They had to throw soft balls at a pile of empty tins. They had to knock six tins off the shelf to win three goldfish. All the children took part, and hey presto! six tins came tumbling off the shelf. The clown handed the children a goldfish each.

"One is named Splish, one is named Splosh, and one is named Splash," he said.

"That is perfect," said Miss Sums.

"Have a nice day," said the clown, smiling and waving.

The children waved back. They then walked back to the carousel and got back on to the gleaming horses, and the horses galloped round and round and up and down and flew into the air.

Suddenly they were back where they started, and they walked back through the archway into the shop.

Mabble Merlin asked if they had enjoyed the carousel ride.

The children shouted excitedly, "YES!"

It had been the best day ever.

Miss Sums thanked Mabble Merlin profusely. She said she couldn't thank him enough. He handed Miss Sums the clock and said Erica was now as good as new; she had just swallowed a bit of soapy water, and no other damage had been done.

Erica English felt very happy. She was looking forward to going back to the school in Osmotherley, now that she could tick and tock perfectly again.

The children were looking forward to telling their classmates about their ride on the carousel, and the other rides at the fairground, and about winning the stuffed toys and the goldfish.

When Miss Sums handed out the stuffed toys to each of the pupils in the class, there were enough for everyone. The paper bag of Liquorice Allsorts that Mabble Merlin had given Miss Sums never seemed to get any emptier – and the three children were never naughty again. Miss Sums was very pleased about that – and so was Erica English, the pretty wall clock.

Milly Paris Enjoys Herself at Tick-Tock School

Milly Paris was really enjoying herself at Tick-Tock School, learning to tick and tock to an excellent standard without missing a beat. Some of the other clocks were bold and beautiful, some were old and just didn't work any more, and some were brand new. The newest clocks at Tick-Tock School learnt to tick-tock and to say their times tables and gained experience of real live numbers.

Milly really liked her room and her little bed in the clock dormitory. Every day she had to visit the clock hospital to have goose fat applied to her hands.

One day she visited the beauty salon to have her face painted by a beautician, and as she lay on the treatment couch getting her face powdered and rouge applied she wondered how Claudette de Seconds was getting along. She wondered if Claudette de Seconds was missing the French court and if she had now grown used to applying her own make-up.

Isaac Newton, a grandfather clock from the British Museum, was at the school to learn Newton's law of gravity. Other clocks had come from all over the world – Germany, France, Italy, America . . . One Italian clock, Leon di Capri, wanted to learn English; a French clock, Jean de Lune, wanted to learn about astrology; a clock from Spain, Gabriella Cadiz, wanted to learn to dance flamenco. . . . There were so many different clocks that every day was like a social whirlwind – especially at lunchtime, when everyone got a chance to chat.

A grandfather clock named Arthur Actor had come from a London theatre in Petticoat Lane to learn mime and dance. He wanted to perform on a big stage one day.

A friendly clock named Piccadilly Moon wanted to learn to sing.

Percy Pudding was a clock from a bakery in Pudding Lane, and he wanted to learn to sing and dance. Percy was a real charmer. There had been a fire in the bakery (someone named Harold Cook had burnt a walnut cake) and Percy Pudding had inhaled too much smoke and had fallen off the wall. The fire brigade came and put the fire out, but Percy Pudding could no longer tick or tock. The baker had brought him to the Tick-Tock School to be repaired after one of his customers handed him Mabble Merlin's business card.

A clock named Shoreditch and a clock named Bow Bells both wanted to learn drama.

A clock named Angus Fisher was from a fishmonger's in Montrose in Scotland.

Tick-Tock School was very difficult, but all the clocks were friendly and polite to Milly when they met during tea breaks and lunchtimes. She felt very at home and comfortable.

She couldn't possibly learn the names of all of them, as there were so many, but she got on well with them all.

One of the new clocks was named Angelica Abracadabra. She came from Aberdeen in Scotland, and a clock named Pauline Skye came from the Isle of Skye. A kitchen clock, Georgette Giles, came from Glencoe in the Highlands. Emma Lou Harris came from the Isle of Lewis, and Matthew Mull was a handsome clock from the Isle of Mull, in Scotland.

There was also a clock from the Lake District. She was from a log cabin, and her name was Amanda Kendal.

William Ness, a clock from Loch Ness, had a picture of Nessie painted on him.

Benjamin Tweed from Berwick-upon-Tweed was a boat clock, and he had fallen into the water when the boat he lived on was being renovated.

Peter Pateley from Pateley Bridge in North Yorkshire was a farm clock. He'd fallen into a peat bog when the farmer and his wife were painting their kitchen. Their son, Hadley Hawk, had put the clock and some furniture in a tractor trailer to take them to a barn so they would be out of the way whilst they were decorating, and somehow Peter had fallen off the trailer.

Christopher Moffat had come from Moffat in Scotland to learn to speak Spanish; Patsy Peebles and Thomas Elgin from Elgin in Scotland were learning French and German.

Diana Dorchester came from Dorchester; Gavin Glossop and Bethany Buxton came from the Peak District; Madison Marple came from a small place near Stockport. These clocks were learning to sing and dance.

Milly was flabbergasted to meet so many clocks. When she went to bed in her little bunk bed in the Tick-Tock School dormitory, she was so tired that she fell fast asleep at once, and she dreamt she could tick-tock perfectly and the Laugherty family were very impressed.

Birthday Presents

Back at the Laugherty household, Claudette de Seconds was holding court and enjoying her conversations with George. George wanted to know all about life at the French court. But the more Claudette talked about life at Marie Antoinette's court the more she missed it, and she dreamt about it when she went to sleep. In fact, she tended to wake up in the night, and then she would wake up George to talk about the French court. Unfortunately, George regularly nodded off, so she had to talk to Omega Horizon instead.

Omega Horizon missed Milly and was always wondering about her.

Mog Og had told all of the clocks what had happened to Milly, so Mog Og became their hero – he could do no wrong! This really pleased Mog Og.

On 31 October it was Halloween. It was also Penelope's birthday.

When Penelope came down for breakfast the children were already up, and they wished her a happy birthday. Then they gave her a charm bracelet and the gift voucher for the Magical Mystery Tour. She was over the moon.

"Oh, the charm bracelet is just so beautiful!" she exclaimed.

"Oh, and all the charms have special powers so that should be fun," said Daisy.

"It certainly will," said Penelope.

"How cool is that!" said Oliver.

"Which lucky charm do you like the best?" asked Daisy.

"Erm, I think I like the magic fairy the best of all."

"So do I," said Daisy.

Miles came into the kitchen.

"Happy birthday, Penelope," he said. "Here is another gift for you." It was a bottle of French wine from the 1920s. "That's definitely going to be strong," he said.

He'd bought it from Mabble Merlin's shop when he bought the silverware. It said on the label 'Chateau Nouveau Vin, 1923', and it didn't cost £500 as it would have done from the local wine shop.

"Gosh!" said Penelope. "Where did you get this from? The guests will be so impressed with this."

"Well, don't be worried about drinking it, as there is more where this came from, I do believe."

Then Patrick came into the kitchen.

"Happy birthday, darling Penelope," he said.

He kissed her on both cheeks and handed her a present. He knew she liked perfume, so he had purchased some brand-new fragrance.

She opened the gift – a small box wrapped in gold paper with a silver bow. She had a feeling it would be perfume and and she was right. It was called Secret Laughter. Patrick had purchased it from the Musty Old Magical Curiosity Shop when he purchased the picture clock. He had never before seen the fragrance on the market, because it wasn't available anywhere else.

Penelope took it out of the box and sprayed some on, and she laughed happily.

"Hey, I could be attracted to you all over again with that fragrance," Patrick said, and they both laughed some more.

No wonder it was called Secret Laughter!

The Cocktail Party Begins

On the evening of the cocktail party, Patrick and Penelope went upstairs to get changed. Their outfits were hanging up in their wardrobes.

Patrick put his 1920s suit on and looked in the mirror. He looked exactly like someone from the 1920s – and for a moment he imagined that he was F. Scott Fitzgerald (a famous writer from the 1920s). He wondered if the suit had once been his. He just didn't know. Then he put his hands in the pockets of the jacket and he realised there was something in each pocket. From the left pocket he pulled out something in blue wrapping paper. It was oblong, and there was a gift tag which said, 'To Patrick, with the compliments of Mabble Merlin'. Patrick was speechless. He immediately unwrapped it and revealed a lovely watch, worth about £3,000. The watch was named Karl Kobex, and it was a twin – but Patrick didn't know that. Karl was from another galaxy – somewhere way past the Crab Nebula and way past the Milky Way. Karl was from somewhere near the Cat's Eye Nebula, which is 3,000 light years away and looks like a cat's eye.

Karl and his twin were able to tell the time in several galaxies, and they had hidden mechanisms which could locate the Musty Old Magical Curiosity Shop. A tiny key was needed to wind up the mechanism, which was hidden in the back of the watch.

The object in Patrick's right pocket was oblong and

wrapped in pink paper. It too had a little gift tag, and this one read, 'To Penelope, happy birthday'. Patrick decided to give it to Penelope as a birthday present from himself. He didn't know for sure, but it was exactly the same size as the box his watch came in so he guessed it was another expensive watch.

He quickly put Karl Kobex on his wrist and gave himself a splash of aftershave. Now he was ready for the party.

Penelope was wearing a 1920s flapper-style dress. It was turquoise with a turquoise boa and silver shoes. She also wore the Egyptian necklace, which was of lapis lazuli. With her long blonde hair she looked like someone from the 1920s, and when she looked into the mirror for a fleeting moment she imagined she was Dorothy Parker (a writer from the 1920s).

Patrick stood in the bedroom doorway.

"Well, doll, are you ready?" he asked.

Penelope looked at Patrick. He looked really spiffing in his pinstriped suit with his sage-green velvet bow tie.

Daisy and Oliver hadn't seen anyone wearing 1920s clothes before, and when they saw their parents they were very impressed.

All the guests began to arrive, and they too were dressed elegantly. The ladies wore beautiful 1920s cocktail dresses with long strings of fancy beads, feathers in their hair, long feather boas and fancy high-heeled shoes. Their dresses were decorated with sequins and tassels. Many of the gentlemen wore moustaches, stuck on with plenty of glue. They had cut their hair short and slicked it down with a side parting. They wore spats, black-and-white shoes, bow ties or cravats, and 1920s suits with waistcoats and pocket watches.

Some arrived in 1920s cars. A black Buick pulled up outside the house, and a 1920 charabanc brought several guests. These cars were hired. They were real vintage cars. Patrick and Penelope had invited forty-eight guests altogether. They were Kitty and Kevin Fishwick, Harriet and Henry Nelson Bollinger, Alice and Karl Bridges, June and Jessie Jakes, Marilyn and Mervin Moor, Henrietta and Herbert Rufus, Belinda and Barry Winters, Charmaine and Charles Sayre, Joyce and Clifford Jones, Beatrice and Brian Brewster, Wanda and Walter Montgomery, Jenny Reach, Abigail Ainsley, Sandra Southern, Michelle Mendip, Carolyn and Andrew Chivers, Cathy Coin, Eric Babbington, Madeleine and Mike Short, Irene and Tom Calvin, John Vermont, Tamara Tolken, Susan Lawrence, Edward Larkin, Bob Fox, Raj Peshwari, Amelia French, Mark Sedgwick, Anthony Pool, Chantelle Chance, Geoffrey Barker and Cherry Scrimshaw.

Miles the butler showed the guests into the house and offered them drinks.

Patrick went into the living room and gave Penelope the gift that he'd found in his pocket.

"Another gift for you, darling," he said.

"Oh, thank you," she said. "I wasn't expecting another one."

He felt like saying, "Neither was I," but instead he said, "You're worth it."

She opened the gift, and it was Katie Kobex – the female twin of Karl Kobex.

"Oh, gosh! Oh, gosh!" Penelope gasped. "This must have cost you a fortune, Patrick."

"Well, look at this," he replied, and he showed Penelope his brand-new wristwatch, which was a twin to hers.

"Oh, my word!" she exclaimed.

"I thought it would be nice to have both of them," he said, "because they are twins."

"Oh, twin souls like you and me, Patrick!" said Penelope.

"Well, something like that," said Patrick. He wanted to say, "Actually, I just found them in the pocket of the jacket I'm wearing, and for all I know they may once have belonged to the original owner of the suit," but he kept quiet.

He thought, 'What would anyone else do if it was his wife's birthday and he found an expensive watch gift-wrapped in his pocket with his wife's name on it, just ready to be opened.'

Miles showed everyone to their seats to the dining room. Bob Fox, who was a film producer, was sitting with his actor friend Raj Peshwari.

Bob Fox piped up: "Where did you get my suit? I just love it."

Patrick answered, "Miles got them for us. You can keep it – it's yours."

"All the outfits look splendid," said Cathy Coin. "They're so elegant!"

"And I love the pocket watch," said Raj Peshwari.

Raj was a handsome man, and he loved the fine things in life, including good-quality clothes. He had real style and people admired him for it.

Henry Nelson Bollinger drank a few glasses of the potent wine that Penelope had been given for her birthday. He became a bit tipsy.

Then the food arrived. There was wild goose in port sauce, asparagus, julienned carrots, butternut squash, potato croquettes and artichoke hearts. For those who didn't want goose there was wild Scottish salmon with mustard sauce and a medley of organic vegetables in ginger-and-apple sauce. Glasses of organic pear wine were served with the meal. For dessert there were strawberry sorbet and wild-strawberry-and-passion-fruit blancmange and chocolate-and-peppermint-chip cookies and wild cherries. Afterwards all the guests were offered pink champagne.

"The food is fabulous," said Harriet.

"There will be a finger buffet later," said Miles. "There's cheese, pickled onions, dips, cocktail sausages, cheese biscuits and an assortment of sandwiches."

"I just love buffet food," said Beatrice.

"I do too," said Belinda.

"I love food," said Karl.

They all laughed.

"Oh, and I must thank you for the watch I found in my pocket," said Karl. "It is in perfect condition, but it looks like a watch from the 1920s. In fact, it's got '1924' on the back of it. It is named Squire Hedges."

Mabble Merlin had put watches in every gentleman's jacket pocket, and in every lady's handbag he'd put a necklace, a bracelet, earrings and a watch.

"I love my watch," said Chantelle Chance.

Hers was a pink watch with a circle of diamonds around

the clock face. This watch was named Fay Diamonds. All the watches had magical powers, but none of the guests knew this. They would all find out in time. The diamonds on Fay Diamond were pink diamonds, hand-mined in South Africa. The motto on the watch was 'Diamonds are a girl's best friend.'

Anthony Pool sat opposite Chantelle. The diamonds sparkled and she was sparkling.

"That watch sparkles like you do," he said.

"Thank you, Anthony. That's a lovely compliment. You look very cute in that suit and with that pocket watch," said Chantelle.

"My grandfather had a pocket watch and I always wanted one. This could be the fashion of the future, don't you think, Chantelle?" he replied.

"What are you talking about?" asked Bob Fox.

"Fashions of the future," said Chantelle.

"Well, let's talk about it, then. Do you think we should go into business and bring out some new fashion designs based on the 1920s and 1930s?"

"I think trilbies and spats should come back into fashion," said Anthony. "And I want boas and feathers and tassels and the charleston dance to come back into fashion."

"Ah," said Bob Fox, "let's call our company Charleston Fashions."

"That's a deal!" said Chantelle enthusiastically.

Elegance was Chantelle's middle name – Chantelle Elegance Chance.

A Game of Cluedo

After the meal, the guests played Cluedo – a game where someone has to murder someone (only pretend, of course) and in some strange way. They chose death by chocolate cake, and Madeleine Short was chosen to be the unlucky victim – only pretend, of course, and all in fun.

Miles had baked a beautiful chocolate cake. He named it 'midnight chocolate cake'. It was laced with rum, but one slice was laced with something stronger – deadly nightshade! It was actually just wild-turkey whisky, but Madeleine had to pretend it was poisonous. Madeleine Short (or Maddy, as she liked to be known) was told to take a bite or two and then pretend to drop down dead.

Miles brought out the chocolate cake, and all the guests thought it was delicious.

"The taste of rum in this is delicious," said Barry Winters.

"Crikey!" croaked Madeleine Short. "I can't taste rum. It's burning my throat. It's like firewater."

Then she dropped to the floor like a bag of hammers. She wasn't really dead – it was just a game – but Mog Og hadn't really understood it was a game. He started to panic.

"Call a doctor!" cried Herbert Rufus. "I think she's been poisoned."

Jessie Jakes rushed over to the 1920s telephone. It was one of those telephones with a separate earpiece, and it looked a bit strange to Mog Og, who couldn't understand what everyone was up to. He was getting a bit worried by this game of Cluedo.

Jessie called a doctor, and seconds later the door burst open and in flew Patrick's friend Dr Rama Singh.

"I'm so glad you could make it, Dr Singh," said Patrick. "We think Madeleine's been poisoned, but we don't know who is responsible."

"Well, it wasn't me," said Mog Og. (Everyone seemed to be looking at him.)

"Sorry, but I think you did it, Mike," said John Vermont.

"I haven't murdered Madeleine. How preposterous!" said Mike Short, seething with anger.

"Someone here must have brought some deadly poison with them, so let's look for it. The bottle must be hidden somewhere."

All the guests went to search for the deadly poison.

Henry Bollinger was getting rather drunk. He went into the living room and noticed the picture clock. It showed Westminster Bridge and Big Ben. Suddenly, the picture changed, so it now showed the London Eye. Then the picture changed again. This time it showed a theatre called the Big Eye, and when he looked closely he could see that there was a date on the building. It read, 'Built in 2012'. He blinked and when he opened his eyes the picture had gone back to the original scene, showing Westminster Bridge and Big Ben. Henry thought he had imagined the whole thing because he'd had too much to drink.

At that moment Harriet came into the room.

"Henry Nelson, you're wobbling," she said. "You have had too much to drink."

"I was just looking at this picture, Harriet, and . . ." Henry was slurring his words.

"Don't tell me – the picture changed and you saw some pink elephants!"

"No, I saw a theatre named the Big Eye, built in 2012."

"Well, Henry, it's not there now, is it?"

Then Alice Bridges came into the room.

"Wow! That is a lovely picture clock of Westminster Bridge," she said.

There were red double-decker buses going over the bridge. It looked like the image was suspended in time, and that's exactly what all the pictures were: real images suspended in time.

Whilst they were admiring London Melody, Dr Rama Singh and Miles helped to carry Madeleine Short upstairs, and they laid her on the spare bed in one of the guest rooms.

Then Dr Rama Singh and Miles went downstairs and Dr Rama Singh said to the assembled guests, "I cannot find a pulse, so it is very bad news. She must have had a great deal of poison to die so quickly."

Then Patrick asked, "Are you off duty now, Dr Singh? Would you like a drink?"

"Of course I'm off duty, Patrick! What do you think I am – a workaholic?"

"Ha ha!" said Patrick. "That's so funny. Would you like a pear wine, my good friend?"

"A pear wine would be excellent."

Dr Singh's wife, Chandra Singh, was in India visiting relatives. She was in Bombay, but she would be going to a hotel named the Jewel of India, in Goa. Dr Singh spent hours on the phone to Chandra, speaking in Gujarati. His phone bill was astronomical.

"Your pear wine, Dr Singh."

As usual, Dr Singh was on his mobile phone, speaking to his wife. Raj Peshwari could understand what he was talking about as he spoke the same language.

"I'm drinking pear wine," Dr Singh told his wife. "Madeleine Short has dropped down dead, and Miles and I have just taken her upstairs and put her on the spare bed in the guest room."

His wife must have said something like "What are you talking about? Are you losing your marbles?" because Dr Singh replied, "No, I'm not losing my marbles. I've got them all. I can't explain now, but it's connected with a game of Cluedo they're playing at Penelope's birthday party, Chandra."

Raj Peshwari was waiting till Dr Singh finished the conversation. He hoped to strike up a conversation with him in Gujarati, but Dr Singh had a great deal to say to his wife so Raj went to speak to Cherry Scrimshaw instead.

Cherry was sitting in the living room, and she had just given Mog Og a pickled onion.

"I see you've finished your drink. Shall I get you another one?" Raj asked.

"Yes, that would be nice," said Cherry.

"What would you like?"

"Irish mead would be nice."

"Shall I bring you a few pickled onions and some party sausage rolls and some pineapple and cheese? It looks like you've been feeding half of yours to Mog Og."

Meanwhile, upstairs Madeleine Short was sitting on the bed, wondering if they had found the bottle of poison or if they had forgotten about her. She thought she'd wait another ten minutes, and she looked at the watch that had come with her necklace and bracelet. It was a gold watch with a gold strap, and it looked as though there were rubies in the strap and a triangle of rubies in the watch face. The watch was named Ruby Sanctuary.

Madeleine fiddled with the watch and pressed some of the buttons on the back. Suddenly the glass covering the watch face swung away and a red beam of light shot out. Unbelievably, it formed a doorway of red light.

Madeleine wondered if she'd been drinking too much or if she was dreaming; something compelled her to walk through the strange door, and she was flabbergasted to find herself in a town she didn't know. She could hear a lot of seagulls so she knew it must be near the sea. She looked at her watch and the glass was back in place.

Well, she walked along and then came to a small building with a sign which read, 'Jezebel's Jazz Club, appearing for one night only, the one and only Madeleine Short'.

Madeleine had always wanted to be a jazz singer, but her singing was a bit rusty as she and her husband had been running their own business non-stop. They owned Bollinger's Fashion House, and they taught designers in the fashion industry, but Madeleine had always wanted to sing jazz in a nightclub.

When she went in, the manager of Jezebel's Jazz Club came over to her and said, "Thank God you're not late!"

"But I'm – I'm—" Madeleine started to stutter.

"Yes, you're here, and that's all that matters," the manager interrupted her.

Suddenly Madeleine felt as if she was a famous jazz singer. She sang a few notes and her voice was incredible. To cut a long story short, that was how Madeleine came to be a jazz singer for a night.

Meanwhile, Miles had gone into the room where he had left Madeleine, but of course she wasn't there. Miles looked under the bed and in the wardrobe and in the en-suite room, but there was no sign of Madeleine.

He went downstairs to tell Mike Short.

"Mike, Madeleine has disappeared into thin air," he said.

"Well, let's go and find her, then," said Mike.

All the guests went searching all over the house, thinking it was part of the game. Little did they realise she was in Folkestone, in Jezebel's Jazz Club — singing instead of pretending to be murdered in a daft game of Cluedo.

As Madeleine enjoyed herself in the jazz club, belting out jazz songs with a group of jazz musicians, the guests were searching high and low for her. They looked under the beds and in the wardrobes and cupboards, and even in the creepy cellar and the loft.

At last Henry Bollinger piped up: "Let's not spoil the party by looking for someone that obviously doesn't want to be found. Game over!"

Mog Og Is Reassured

At the end of the first song Madeleine felt fantastic. The crowd had really enjoyed it. One of the revellers came over and asked where Madeleine had got her lovely 1920s dress.

She had forgotten that she was wearing an authentic 1920s dress. It was a sparkly crimson dress with a red feather boa and sparkly red shoes – the perfect dress for a singer in a jazz club.

Mog Og decided he'd had enough party food. He was worried about Madeleine. He couldn't get his head round it – first she was dead, then she disappeared, but how, and why, and where to?

He decided to ask Polly Quazar. He wanted to know what in the world was going on. Did anybody know?

"Hey, Polly Quazar," shouted Mog Og. (It was so noisy in the house with all the guests running around.) "I'd just like to know what's happened to Madeleine. Have you got any ideas? Was she really murdered?"

"Of course she wasn't murdered, Mog Og. It was just a game."

"Well, where has she gone to?"

"Well, she's alive and well and happy and in Folkestone."

"In Folkestone!" yelled Mog Og. "Stop kidding around, Polly."

"I don't know how she got there, but I know she is there. She's in a jazz club singing."

"Will she be back?"

"Oh, yeah, Mog Og, she'll be back."

"Don't tell me – before midnight!" yelled Mog Og. "And who murdered her in the game?"

"Actually it was the very beautiful Cherry Scrimshaw. She worked for Bollinger's Fashion House near Hampstead and she was furious when they chose Sandra Southern's designs instead of hers," said Polly.

"Well, that's very mean of Cherry Scrimshaw. She was feeding me pickled onions all night, so I'm lucky she didn't try to poison me too."

"The game is only pretend, Mog Og. It isn't real – it's just for fun," said Polly, shouting above the noise.

"So where has Madeleine gone if, as you say, it's just a game."

"As I said, Mog Og, Madeleine will be—"

"Back before midnight?" interrupted Mog Og.

"Exactly!" said Polly. "I rest my case."

"Well, I'd better take my confused brain out and put my clear brain back in, because later tonight I've got a date with a lovely lady feline."

"Anyone we know?" asked Polly.

"Her name's Mystique."

More Broken Clocks

The guests had given up looking for Madeleine, and they were all settled back at the table waiting to be served with individual jellies. Miles brought them on a tray.

"I'll help you to hand them out," piped up Henry Bollinger, who was even more tipsy than before.

He took a few off the tray, but he was so unsteady, and the jelly wibbled and wobbled so much, that one fell down the back of Marilyn's dress. She was wearing a beautiful silver dress – she looked like a mermaid.

"Wha-woo!" she screamed. "That's cold!"

The other guests started to laugh as Miles rushed forward with a napkin.

"Don't worry," said Marilyn.

Mervin took the napkin off Miles and used it to wipe jelly from the back of her dress.

"I'm awfully sorry," said Henry. "I'm a huge clumsy oaf."

"You can say that again!" said Harriet, and they all laughed.

But out of the jelly had tumbled a little key, and Mervin said, "What's this key for? Perhaps the bottle of poison has been locked away somewhere."

The poison was locked away in a tiny trinket box in the handbag of Cherry Scrimshaw. She had tried to hide the trinket box in the grandfather clock in the hall, but she couldn't open the clock so she had hidden it on a shelf in the closet. Charles Sayre had seen her hiding it, and he had slipped the box back into Cherry's handbag.

Henry grabbed the key as Miles brought in some blancmange.

"Who wants blancmange?" he asked.

Miles stood there with a huge blancmange on a tray.

"That looks gorgeous!" said Tamara.

Suddenly Mervin grabbed the key back off Henry, and as he did so his elbow caught the corner of the tray. The huge blancmange fell off the tray, and some of it landed on Mog Og, some landed on Wanda, some landed on Carolyn Chivers, some on Clifford Jones, some on June Jakes, and some on Charles Sayre.

Mog Og shouted and rushed around the room. At the same time, the cuckoo clock, Jasmine Feathersprings, started to cuckoo. She screeched at Mog Og because as he shook the blancmange off his fur some of it went into her feathers and up her nose, almost choking her, and in her mouth. She coughed and spluttered and shouted at Mog Og until her voice was hoarse.

"I've got a date tonight, and look at the state of me!" shouted Mog Og.

"And look at the state of me!" cried Jasmine. "It's your fault, Mog Og."

She flew out at Mog Og, and her springs suddenly broke. She tried to stand up, but she couldn't. She could hardly speak.

"Oh dear, oh dear! I've broken my feather springs," she gasped. Then she sat down and began to cry.

Meanwhile Mike had found a large key, and he thought he would open George up to see if the deadly nightshade was hidden inside. However, the key was for winding George up, and in his attempt to open the clock he wound poor George so much that he could hardly breathe. Suddenly all George's springs made a loud popping sound, as though something had broken, but he was just wound up so tight he couldn't breathe. He couldn't tick and tock any more, and it looked as though his eyebrows had risen two inches off his face.

"Oh, George, you don't look well," said Mog Og when he came into the hallway.

"Oh, dear! Oh, me!" said George. "I've been wound up too tight. I can hardly breathe."

Miles went upstairs to have one last look for Madeleine. He went in and out of all the bedrooms until he was dizzy. In the bedroom Penelope had used to get ready in he found Omega Horizon on the floor. Her face was cracked, and it looked as though some clumsy oaf had trodden on her. Omega had shouted for help, but then she had passed out with the pain.

Miles picked her up, and then on the dressing table he noticed a business card from Mabble Merlin's Clock-and-Watch Hospital. 'Open all hours – Dial 123456 and we'll be there before you put the phone down,' it read.

Miles carried Omega Horizon downstairs, and he soon realised that the grandfather clock wasn't working. Then he saw that Jasmine wasn't working. And then, when he went into the kitchen, he saw the French court clock, Claudette de Seconds, sitting on the floor. In a fit of temper she'd jumped off the wall. She was sick of all the noise – especially Mog Og running around shouting. She missed life at the French court. One of her hands had fallen off, and she hadn't bothered to put her make-up on or to do her hair. Her false eyelashes had also fallen off.

Miles picked her up off the floor and quickly went to make a phone call. He wasn't thinking straight, and he went to use the pretend 1920s phone, which wasn't even connected.

"Hello," said Miles. "Is that the clock-and-watch hospital?"

"At your service," answered Mabble Merlin.

As soon as Miles put the phone down there was a knock at the door, and Miles and Karl Bridges picked up George and carried him to Mabble Merlin's collection van. Miles then took Jasmine off the wall and handed her to Mabble Merlin. Then he gave him Omega Horizon, and then he handed over Claudette de Seconds.

Mabble Merlin sped off in the van to get them all quickly to hospital, and when they arrived Milly was very pleased to see them all.

Patrick's Early Days

Some of the guests still had room for more sweet, and Miles had fortunately also made a sherry trifle – a very large trifle as this was his favourite sweet. It was tangerine trifle with lots of hundreds and thousands sprinkled on top.

Miles brought in the trifle, and the guests stopped running around so much and started to relax. Patrick and Penelope relaxed too, even though they still hadn't found Madeleine Short.

Patrick recalled that in his early days as a medical student he had a similar experience that he never got to the bottom of when someone he knew disappeared from the face of the earth. In his life, and particularly lately, lots of things had happened that he couldn't explain.

He had a feeling Madeleine would reappear, so he thought he'd keep the guests entertained so they didn't start rushing round the house again, looking for her and standing on watches. At parties he knew there was often one person who was a bit clumsy, and he knew Henry was a bit of a clumsy oaf.

The conversation turned to Patrick's years as a medical student. Like many medical students, he travelled abroad during his seven years' medical training. In the USA, he travelled to Florida with a few friends who were also doing their medical training. They went to see the Kennedy Space Centre, Disney World, and Sea Life Centre.

While he was in Florida, Patrick celebrated his twenty-first birthday – a big reason to celebrate. He chartered a yacht for a week, and he invited his seven friends (Mike, Steve, Robert, Luke, Paul, Simon and Logan) to go with him on a cruise. The yacht was piloted by a Floridian yachtsman named Lance Pitt, a very handsome man with blonde curly hair.

It was great for the first few days. It was sunny and warm, and sometimes there was a cool Floridian sea breeze, deep-blue skies and the relaxed atmosphere of the deep South of America.

On the eve of Patrick's birthday they had a few drinks to celebrate. They had a buffet, told jokes, danced and swam in the sea.

That night, when they were all in their bunks, a strange humming was heard and one of the medical students (an American guy named Robert Walton) went out on deck. He didn't know that the yacht was now in the fabled Bermuda Triangle, just off the coast of Florida. As Robert went out on deck a light beamed down – an eerie blue light – and he was beamed up by the light, never to be seen again.

Next morning the other guests woke up a little later than usual. They still felt a little groggy from the celebration drinks, and they had a bit of a hangover. They didn't realise at first that Robert was missing as they were all a bit groggy that morning, but by midday they knew he had disappeared completely. They were totally shocked.

That same night a yachtswoman named Cassandra Hart was on her father's yacht not far from Patrick Laugherty's boat. She had been woken by a humming noise and had gone out on deck to investigate. She saw Robert Walton come up on deck and an eerie blue light beaming down from a large saucer-shaped object in the dark midnight sky. She too had been celebrating with friends, and she put what she'd seen down to imagination because she was overtired and she'd drunk a few glasses of champagne. She was trying not to smoke, but she had a cigarette and a cup of hot chocolate to calm her nerves before she calmly went back to her bunk.

She was awoken next day by the police who were investigating Robert Walton's disappearance.

Patrick told this strange story to the guests at the cocktail party.

"Do you think he would have made a good doctor?" asked one of Patrick's friends.

"He would have been excellent, but he wanted to go into medical research anyway. He's possibly in another galaxy now, or in a parallel world – or wherever UFOs come from. He was the best."

Patrick had also travelled to the Valley of the Kings in Egypt and also to Machu Pichu in Peru. He had seen the Pyramids, and he had many Egyptian artefacts. In the dining room he had a huge golden sarcophagus. It was standing in the corner of the room. He had some ancient papyruses on the walls, and one of them depicted Tutankhamen and his wife.

Back from the Dead

After Patrick told all the guests his yachting story they wondered if Madeleine Short had disappeared for ever.

Henry said, "I have an idea. I think one of the ladies has the poison in her handbag."

Charles Sayre, who had seen Cherry Scrimshaw hiding the trinket box and had popped it back into her handbag, stood up and said, "Yes, gentlemen, I know who the murderer is. She had the poison in her handbag and still does."

"That's just rubbish," said Cherry.

"Well, will you empty the contents of your handbag on to the table?"

"Of course I will. I've nothing to hide."

Cherry emptied her handbag, and out tumbled the trinket box.

"Oh, my God!" she screamed.

She was a very good actress. In fact, she screamed so loud that Raj Peshwari was shocked. She had seemed so quiet and petite and sweet, but she was suddenly like a wild animal.

"What!" he exclaimed.

Henry had the tiny little key, so he opened the trinket box and there was the bottle of poison.

"So it was you!" exclaimed Raj Peshwari.

He had really liked Cherry, but he wasn't so sure now.

"It's just a game, Raj!"

"But where is Madeleine Short?"

"Crikey, I don't know, Raj! She probably got bored and went home."

"I think I might know," piped up Raj.

Suddenly Dr Rama Singh appeared. He'd finally stopped speaking on the phone. He saved the day by speaking to Raj in Gujarati about his wife in India.

"How are you getting on with Cherry?" asked Rama Singh.

"Well, she murdered Madeleine, so I guess I don't want to be with the murderer."

Dr Singh started to laugh, and he couldn't stop.

"It was just a game," he laughed.

"Well, when Madeleine reappears from out of the wardrobe I'll forgive her."

"OK," said Dr Singh. "Perhaps Cherry could be an actress. That sounds like a good profession for her. What does she do?" he asked.

"She's training to be a doctor."

"I don't think she should with a bottle of poison in her handbag."

"It's only a game, Dr Singh – remember," said Raj Peshwari.

Meanwhile Madeleine Short finished singing in the jazz club, and got ready to leave. She was wondering how she would get home. She walked outside Jezebel's Jazz Club and stood for a few seconds debating what to do. She believed the watch could somehow transport her back.

She was just looking at it, when suddenly a van pulled up and Mabble Merlin got out. He was dressed in 1920s clothes, and as she looked the van was suddenly transformed into a 1920s taxi.

"Are you looking for a lift home, Madeleine?" he asked. "Well, look no further."

Madeleine jumped into the taxi, Mabble Merlin pressed a button and the car whizzed along through the night.

Mabble Merlin asked if Madeleine had enjoyed singing in the nightclub and if it had been a dream come true.

"That was such a blast!" said Madeleine. "I have had the best night ever. But I think Mike will be glad to have me back again, and so will the guests."

The car whizzed down back lanes and round bends, and it hardly touched the road. Madeleine looked out of the car window and noticed a full moon. It was October 31st – Halloween – the night when strange things happen.

Soon Mabble Merlin reached the Laugherty home. He and Madeleine walked up to the front door and rang the doorbell. They could hear the noise of the cocktail party going on inside.

Miles opened the door.

"We've looked high and low for you, Madeleine," he said. "I'm glad to see you."

"Miles, can you just say to the others that I fell asleep upstairs in one of the closets?"

"Of course I can, Madeleine."

Madeleine walked into the room and Mike said, "Oh, hello, honey, I've missed you tonight."

"I fell asleep in the closet upstairs."

"Oh, dear! I thought you must be asleep upstairs somewhere, honey," said Mike.

Cherry turned to Raj Peshwari and said, "Are you happy now Madeleine's back safe and sound?"

"Very happy! So how about you and me?"

"Well, I'm interested in you," said Cherry.

The Two American Tourists

That same Halloween, Cynthia and Tobias Chimes were standing outside the Sands of Time Hotel in Bayswater. It was between a Chinese restaurant called The Blue Oyster, and a French restaurant called The Parisienne.

It was 8.30 in the morning and Tobias and Cynthia, who were on holiday from Brooklyn, New York, were waiting for a taxi to take them to Wiltshire. They wanted to visit the historical sites of Salisbury, Stonehenge and Avebury, and they also hoped to go to a medieval fayre. They were so excited as they waited on the steps in front of the revolving hotel door.

They both looked left and then right, and Cynthia did a double take and looked left again when she saw a shop that she knew for sure wasn't there the night before. If it had been there, they surely would have been in it, as they were looking for souvenirs to take back and it was exactly the kind of shop they had been looking for. It was sandwiched between the Sands of Time Hotel and the French restaurant. They both looked at the shop, then looked at each other.

"Wow!" they said simultaneously. "Wow!" they said again.

They looked at the shop and the name of the shop (the Musty Old Magical Curiosity Shop) and they looked at each other, and they were flabbergasted. Lots of things happen in a big city like New York, but they'd never seen anything like this.

They both spun round and rushed back inside the hotel through the revolving doors to ask the hotel owner, Claude Monet, if he knew there was a Musty Old Magical Curiosity Shop next door.

The hotelier stopped painting for a while and said, "I don't think so." Claude Monet was French and he shrugged his shoulders in a very French way. "But anything is possible in London," he said. "Even the rain can rain upside down!"

Tobias Chimes said in his very loud and broad New York accent, "Well, I'll be blown away by that, but there it is now – right next door."

"Maybe you should take a look around. Tomorrow it may be gone – just like the clouds that sail by," said Claude, and he turned away to finish the painting he was painting.

He wore a beret, a moustache which curled up, a stripy shirt like the ones mime artists wear and trousers with braces. The painting looked like the street outside, complete with the Musty Old Magical Curiosity Shop next to the French restaurant. It also showed the Chinese restaurant on the other side of the hotel. Claude's painting was very good.

The American duo took out their cameras and rushed back outside. They decided there and then to postpone the trip to Stonehenge. Tobias phoned the taxi company, who answered straight away.

"Hey, is that the taxi company, Travelling Light?" asked Tobias.

"Yes, it is."

"Well, Toby and Cindy Chimes won't be going to Stonehenge today. Something unexpected has turned up – real unexpected. We'll put it on ice for a few days."

"OK, as you wish, Mr Chimes. Have a great day," said the man from the taxi company.

Tobias and Cynthia decided to wander around the Musty Old Magical Curiosity Shop for a day or two – or possibly three or four. It occurred to them that they might never come out and that they could end up being whisked up in the shop to another galaxy. They had heard of musty old police boxes that flew through space and travelled far and wide, and they didn't see why a shop shouldn't do the same. Suddenly they wanted a whole new life, travelling around the galaxies and to other universes and maybe travelling back in time. Their imaginations were running riot.

The American duo – 'Calamity Cindy and Tricky Tobias Chimes' – were an adventurous couple. Tobias was a freelance photographer and Cynthia was an artist. She was very creative, and she had studied art, design and drama. Tobias had studied photography and graphic design. They worked for themselves, and recently they had decided to take a year out to gain new experiences. As they travelled, Cynthia sketched and painted and Tobias took photographs. London was the ideal place – enigmatic and lovely. Tobias took some amazing photographs, even in the pouring rain. Londoners didn't bat an eyelid when he took pictures of them.

Tobias had a theory that clones were infiltrating society. He had other theories too. He was quite a philosopher.

He had tousled sandy-blonde hair and glasses, and he had a bit of a tummy on him. With his photography equipment slung over his shoulder, his hat, his baggy trousers and his T-shirt, he looked like a typical New Yorker.

Cynthia had thick blonde hair in a pageboy style and a very nice complexion. She had been brought up in the Blue Ridge Mountains of West Virginia. She used to go horse-riding regularly, but owing to the easy life of painting and drawing, and of course the fridge being too handy, she had put on a few pounds. She loved cakes, cookies, candy . . . in fact, anything sweet, so she was a bit on the plump side.

She had decided to do some very gentle exercises when

she got to London – when she had the time, of course. She had devised an exercise plan and a healthy-eating regime. The exercises were brand-new ones she'd devised after she'd read a t'ai-chi book. From the very simple Chinese exercises detailed in the book, she had created her own system, which she called the Simple Secret Exercise Plan. For example, an exercise for bingo wings (that is, flab on the upper arms) and flab on the front and back of legs was named 'Hitch a Ride' and she explained it like this: firstly, form a fist with both hands as if you are thumbing a lift (fingers tucked into palms and thumbs upright). You get the meaning so far? Then bring your forearms upwards to literally bounce off your upper arms. As you do this action you bend your legs and drop your backbone down – easy-peasy lemon squeezy.

Every now and then Cynthia would do about ten Hitch a Ride repetitions – gentle enough and simple enough to do whilst waiting in the hotel lobby – for instance, whilst Tobias popped out to buy the *London Times*.

It was surprising how the exercises cottoned on with the staff in the hotel, and all the staff seemed to want to learn.

There was also an exercise named 'The Clap' where you clap in front of your leg and then lift up your leg and clap behind your leg. And then there was another exercise named 'The Digger' where you make your hand and arm into the shape of a digger. Your hand would be like a shovel going towards the ground.

Then there was the 'Pluck a Grape from a Vine'. Just imagine this: you have a grapevine and you pluck imaginary grapes from it. Then of course you could crush the grapes, stomping on them. That's good for your feet.

Another good exercise for your feet was 'Roll a Pencil'. You have to imagine you have a pencil under your foot. Cynthia would say, "Imagine you have a pencil under your left foot or right foot and you are rolling the pencil very slowly with your foot. This exercise is for balance. When you get better at it you can imagine you are rolling with a stick of Blackpool rock or even a church candle and see whether you can keep your balance."

Then for neck exercises – so you don't end up with a turtleneck – you can blow a French-style kiss. That is, you move your head as if you were kissing someone on both cheeks. You have to imagine you are kissing a famous person, such as a beautiful pop star (imagining the person in front of you will keep you focused).

Cynthia also had an exercise called 'The Funky Chicken'. You have to walk like a funky farmyard chicken, strutting up and down. At the same time you can sing, "Walk like a funky chicken, drop your backbone down, even though you look ridiculous, you may lose weight and look stupendous." Cynthia would strut up and down in the lobby of the Sands of Time Hotel, and soon enough all the staff and guests would be joining in, strutting up and down like funky chickens. They all thought Cynthia was hilarious.

In this way Cynthia was beginning to lose weight. Every day she was a little bit fitter than before.

Tobias also took part in the exercises. It was amazing how contagious they were.

Cynthia was always cooking up something new, and she was thrilled to think her figure would soon be slimline. Her hair was her best feature – thick and shiny and a lovely shade of blonde. Her skin was glowing – she definitely had good-quality skin and she had lovely twinkling eyes. She thought to herself, 'I'm not a cheap cut of meat.'

Tobias was handsome despite being overweight. He was addicted to anything sweet. He took five sugars in his tea. He definitely had a sweet tooth – or rather, many sweet teeth. He had thought of using honey instead of sugar, but it was just a thought. He loved chocolate, cakes (especially sponge cakes), custard pies and flapjacks.

When he worked as a freelance photographer in New York, he sometimes worked late into the night – sometimes working with other shutter bugs and having late-night snacks at late-night cafés and eating a lot of chocolate bars in the late-night cafés. New York is the city that never goes to sleep. He also loved anything greasy, such as burgers and greasy chips from greasy-spoon cafés. In short, he loved junk food. He thought he should maybe see a hypnotherapist to help him lose weight. He was eating non-stop and it was getting on his nerves.

He hoped that a year's holiday would get him to change his lifestyle and get him away from the American dream of constant cream cakes and chocolate cookies. He needed some self-discipline. He had seen Londoners in films and on the television, and they all seemed so slim in their pinstriped suits and bowler hats and brollies. He had never seen a fat man in a pinstriped suit and bowler hat and carrying a brolly.

Cynthia loved to make quiches and pies. Cherry pie and

apple-and-rhubarb pie were particular favourites. She also baked lovely cakes, and her blueberry muffins were especially good.

Cynthia and Tobias were both in their thirties and they hadn't had any children. They both came from large families. Cynthia's grandmother had eighteen children and her parents had nine children; Tobias was the youngest of thirteen children. They wanted a life before they had children – or, at least, they wanted an adventure.

Their house, however, was always full of other people's children. The only pets they had were fishes, which they kept in a large aquarium. Their third-floor apartment in New York had a panoramic view of the city, and the apartment was full of Tobias's photographs and Cynthia's paintings. When they came to England, they rented their apartment out to two New York fashion designers called Francesca Florence and Dune Passion, who promised to look after their tropical fish.

Tobias reminded the fashion designers that fish only had a three-second memory.

"Oh," said Dune, "is that why they suddenly change direction – because they can't remember where they are going?"

They all laughed, and the two fashion designers wished Cynthia and Tobias a brilliant vacation in England and a safe journey.

The American Duo Travel Through Time

The Musty Old Magical Curiosity Shop was about to take off suddenly into the air, and the American duo were in for a big surprise. They walked into the shop, and they were so excited by all the antiques and things that the shop sold. It was full to the brim – or fuller.

Cynthia and Tobias noticed Mabble Merlin behind the counter of the shop. He was wearing a Victorian suit, and Cynthia and Tobias thought he looked quaint. In fact, the suit was made in the year 1860, and it looked like the kind of suit a doctor might wear.

"This is such a quaint little shop!" said Cynthia. "I never noticed it yesterday. We were just going to take a trip to Stonehenge when we noticed your shop."

"I'm so glad you noticed it," said Mabble Merlin.

"Well, we are from Brooklyn, New York," said Cynthia. "I'm Cindy, and this is my partner in crime, Toby."

"And I'm Mabble Merlin," said Mabble Merlin.

"We're staying next door at the Sands of Time Hotel. We plan to stay in England about a year," said Cynthia in her Brooklyn accent.

"It's a working holiday, you see," said Tobias, chipping in.

"Well," said Mabble Merlin, that's time enough for you to enjoy a real trip. If you are interested, I've got two exclusive tickets for you both for the Magical Mystery Tour."

"An adventure!" said Cynthia excitedly.

"The Magical Mystery Tour sounds awesome," said Tobias in his broad Brooklyn accent.

"Just say yes," said Mabble Merlin, "and we can be on our way right away. There's no need to book it; we'll be off in a second."

"Wow, that's fantastic!" said Tobias.

They both turned to Mabble Merlin, and Cynthia said, "Count us in for the Magical Mystery Tour. We're both on board."

Mabble Merlin said, "That's wonderful. You'll be going somewhere you haven't been before. Give me a few minutes and we'll be off."

Mabble Merlin closed the door of the shop and came back to the shop counter. Cynthia and Tobias looked on as Mabble Merlin pulled a lever and the shop till disappeared beneath the shop counter. He pulled another lever and a space-age-looking console rose up in its place. It was covered with futuristic-looking buttons, lights, flashing numbers, colours and symbols. The lights flashed green, red, orange, blue, yellow, purple and indigo. Suddenly three seats popped up in front of the console panel – just enough seats for Mabble Merlin, Tobias and Cynthia.

"OK, Cindy and Toby, take your seats, fasten your seat belts, recline and take a deep breath."

Cynthia and Tobias were excited and amazed.

"Wow, this is really something!" said Tobias in his broad Brooklyn accent.

"This is so magical!" said Cynthia. "Is it a cyberspace trip, where we look at the screen and just think and feel we're going somewhere?" asked Tobias, trying to figure out what was happening.

"Oh, no – definitely not cyberspace. You can do a cyberspace trip if you want, or we could do the real thing

– a real trip back in time. You choose a date and we'll go back there," said Mabble Merlin.

"You're joking! You're kidding around, Mr Merlin!" said Tobias.

"No, I'm not kidding around. If you want to go, your wish is my command."

"OK," said Tobias, slowly taking in the information. "Personally I just love the Tudors – anything to do with King Henry VIII. It would be awesome to go back to that historical period."

"Yes, I also love the Tudors – anything to do with Anne Boleyn. I just love the way they dressed in that era, and I love their passion and enthusiasm for life."

"Well, that's a deal," said Mabble Merlin.

His mud-brown eyes sparkled and twinkled. He definitely liked the idea of the Tudor era himself. When Cynthia and Tobias turned again to look at Mabble Merlin he was no longer wearing his old Victorian suit; he was now wearing a pointed purple hat with strange symbols swirling on it and around it as if they were alive, which of course they were. It was as if the hat was helping Mabble Merlin to think – and indeed it was a very intelligent thinking cap, and it was helping him to concentrate on going back in time.

The long purple robe that Mabble Merlin was now wearing was also covered in similar strange symbols; they made Cynthia and Tobias feel woozy.

Tobias piped up: "OK, let's do it. I'm going to choose the year 1533 – a good year for the Tudors."

"Right then," said Mabble Merlin, becoming excited at the thought of going back to that year. "Toby, please tap the year into the control panel."

Tobias's hand was shaking. He felt scared and excited at the same time. Already he could almost see Henry VIII coming alive before him. He could almost hear the music from the court and hear the laughter.

Tobias steadied his hand and carefully tapped the digits 1-5-3-3 into the control panel. Then Mabble Merlin instructed the two travellers to recline in their chairs. After a few seconds the shop began to make a strange whooshing, popping and gurgling noise. It was ever so strange, like the noises of some underground world. After a few more strange noises the shop suddenly whizzed upwards. It was better than being on an aeroplane. Cynthia's and Tobias's tummies did somersaults as the shop went faster and faster – much faster than an aeroplane, that's for sure.

Cynthia and Tobias gripped their seats. They didn't dare speak. They wondered if they had made a huge mistake. The lights and numbers on the control panel were flashing, and beeping noises combined with the whooshing, popping, gurgling and whizzing. Gradually something became visible on a screen in front of them. They saw the outlines of towns and cities getting further away and then they saw an ocean – it looked like the Pacific Ocean. By now they were miles and miles up in the air.

Suddenly they began to slow down until they were just drifting upwards, and now there was very little noise.

Cynthia's heart was beating fast and Tobias was so excited he could hardly breathe.

Mabble Merlin said, "We have now left the earth's atmosphere and we're heading for deep space."

Then a very soothing feminine voice came over the speaker: "We are now leaving the earth's atmosphere and heading for deep space, Captain Mabble Merlin," the voice said.

Cynthia and Tobias were glad to hear another voice. It somehow convinced them that they were actually on a real cosmic trip.

"Do you require drinks, Captain Mabble Merlin?" said

the soothing voice over the speakers. This was obviously the cosmic air hostess, and suddenly she appeared on the screen. Cynthia and Tobias expected her to look artificial, like an android, but she was very human-looking except that her eyes were turquoise and she had small crystals over her eyebrows and over her temples. She also had hair like blonde candyfloss.

"Hello, Xanadu. It's very nice to see you today," said Mabble Merlin. "Yes, we would like three mineral juice drinks, please – with booster, please, Xanadu."

"Yes, Captain," replied Xanadu Crystal.

Three tall glasses instantly materialised on the counter as if by magic. They were all different colours and fizzing like lemonade.

"Wow!" said Tobias. "They look great, but what is the booster?"

"Oh, that's magnesium, rare minerals and plankton, so you can acclimatise your nervous system to space travel."

"Oh, I suppose I do need something like that," said Tobias with a laugh.

"Which one is mine?" asked Cynthia.

"Yours is the purple one, Cindy. It's got purple chlorophyll in it. Believe it or not, chlorophyll, which is what makes grass green, was at one time purple. And, Toby, the green one is yours. That's the colour of plankton, fresh from the Pacific Ocean. The pink juice, which is mine, has pink coral in it. It is very good for bones and teeth. The pink coral was harvested from the Great Barrier Reef. We will be drinking these mineral juice drinks with added boosters throughout the trip."

"Sounds cool!" said Tobias, before taking a sip of his. "This juice tastes delicious. It tastes a bit like kiwi fruit and lime."

"It's quite possible that it has those fruits in it," said Mabble Merlin.

"Wow!" said Cynthia after taking a sip of her juice. "Mine tastes like bilberries and plums, and there's a coconut taste too."

"Possibly there's a bit of coconut milk in there as coconut milk is perfectly balanced," said Mabble Merlin.

Mabble Merlin sipped his through a straw.

"Hmm," he said, "that tastes as good as it looks. I can taste peaches, strawberries, Chinese gooseberries and cherries."

The exotic drinks relaxed them, which is what they were designed to do. They were no longer so nervous about their trip into the unknown.

"Where does Xanadu Crystal come from?" asked Tobias.

"And who does she work for?" asked Cynthia.

"Well, Xanadu comes from the constellation of Pegasus."

"Oh, yes," said Tobias, "I know about Pegasus from Greek mythology. Pegasus was the winged horse. He was born from the body of Medusa, the gorgon, when she was decapitated by Perseus."

"Oh, yes," said Cynthia, "my Greek mythology is coming back to me now."

"And in the midnight sky Pegasus is right next to Andromeda. It is the seventh largest constellation in the sky," said Tobias. "It's a square with three tendrils from it," he said as he drew it in mid-air.

On the plasma screen above the control panel the night sky appeared complete with the constellation of Pegasus.

"To answer your second question," said Mabble Merlin, "Xanadu works for the Magical Mystery Tours Corporation – working for you, working for us. As you can see, Cindy, Toby, we're a large and reputable corporation."

"Relax back in your seats and just enjoy your trip," said the voice of Xanadu Crystal.

"Oh, boy, this is some trip!" said Tobias. "I feel very relaxed and dreamy now."

"So do I," said Cynthia.

"We are now entering deep space," said Mabble Merlin.

Then on the plasma screen there appeared what looked like the whole of the cosmos – it certainly looked like deep space – and a voice announced, "This is Deep Earth calling." (A cosmic-looking man appeared on the screen.) "Hi, Captain. This is Quantum Phoenix."

"Hi, Quantum," said Mabble Merlin.

"You are now going through deep space. Please enjoy the scenery," said Quantum.

"He looks very cosmic," said Cynthia.

His skin looked smooth and flawless and his hair was very blonde.

"Yes," said Mabble Merlin, he's from Cygnus Xi. Cygnus Xi is a neutron star," he explained.

"Oh," said Cynthia, "I didn't know anyone lived on neutron stars."

"Well," said Mabble Merlin, "they are very useful places as they have many wormholes, through which you can travel backwards in time. Wormholes are like cosmic motorways."

"That sounds like science fiction," said Tobias.

"Well, it's actually science fact," replied Mabble Merlin.

"Have we far to go?" asked Cynthia.

"We have to pass through this wormhole of Cygnus Xi, and then we will land in the year 1533, as you wished, Toby."

"Oh, that's just incredible," said Tobias excitedly.

"We'll have some more refreshments and a light lunch," said Mabble Merlin.

Mabble Merlin pressed a button and Quantum Phoenix came back on to the plasma screen.

"How can I help, Captain," he asked.

"Can I order three cosmic pizzas?"

Suddenly the three pizzas arrived. They were Crab

Nebula pizzas with space-dust toppings, and there were also three large drinks and each of them was a different colour. This time Mabble Merlin had a yellow drink, Tobias had an orange drink and Cynthia had a blue drink.

"This pizza is delicious," said Cynthia.

"And my drink is lovely," said Tobias.

"Yes, they do serve good food. You need to eat well if you are travelling backwards in time through wormholes. These are seafood pizzas, and the topping is full of mineral salts," said Mabble Merlin. "Now just relax and enjoy the view of deep space. We will soon be heading towards earth in the year 1533."

Cynthia and Tobias relaxed into their seats to enjoy the views of space and the view of 1 million stars twinkling. The view seemed endless, and it was making them feel sleepy.

Suddenly the plasma screen flickered and they could now see Planet Earth — a blue planet. They could see the land and the ocean, and they were zooming closer with every second. Soon they could see London. They assumed it was London, though there were no cars and no high-rise buildings. There was plenty of smoke, and there were plenty of trees and pastureland. They could see men on horseback galloping.

Then the voice of Quantum Phoenix came over the speakers: "We are now arriving on earth in 1533, the Tudor era. King Henry VIII is on the throne. Have a nice trip."

"Thank you, Quantum," said Mabble Merlin.

"How will we manage without hot running water and flushing toilets," Cynthia asked.

"And we won't have televisions, telephones, radios or fridges," said Tobias.

"And what about a bed to sleep in? I think Tudor beds will be uncomfortable, so we may end up with bad backs," said Cynthia.

"Don't worry about that," said Mabble Merlin. "You will be staying in the accommodation above this shop. You are in room 103, with en-suite shower and bathroom, hot running water and room service."

"Can we take our mobile phones with us?" asked Tobias.

"Well, they won't work, but I will give you both a wristwatch communicator. You can use them to talk to me or to the Magical Mystery Tours headquarters if you need to."

"Can I take my camera with me?" asked Tobias.

"Yes, you can, as long as no one sees it. I will give you a satchel with a secret pocket to keep it in."

"Can I make sketches or paint and take my easel?" asked Cynthia.

"Yes, I think that will be fine," said Mabble Merlin, "but remember pens were not invented in 1533 so be a little discreet. If you have any problems, use your communicators and help will be on hand."

Suddenly there was a jolt and the shop landed opposite Hampton Court in Abbot's Lane, between a dressmaker's owned by Mrs Greensleeves and a tavern named The Partridge in a Pear Tree. They had arrived.

Room 103

Where the shop had landed there had been a baker's shop called The Baker's Dozen. The shop owner, Hector Spice, had sold the shop as he wanted to expand the business. He had gone to Tintagel and opened a very large baker's shop selling Cornish pasties. It was named The Cornish Pasty. He married a girl in Cornwall named Rachel Rendezvous, whose father was French and very wealthy.

Mabble Merlin landed his shop in the empty space where Hector Spice's bakery had been.

The Partridge in a Pear Tree was owned by Bartholomew Mead and his wife, Eleanor Mead.

Cynthia and Tobias couldn't wait to step outside the shop and explore, but they couldn't go out in the clothes they had on. They had to wear the clothes of Tudor times.

Mabble Merlin went into one of his storerooms and when he came out he was dressed in a green velvet outfit.

He told Cynthia and Tobias he would go to Mrs Miranda Greensleeves' dressmaker's shop and purchase them some brand-new costumes.

Mabble Merlin popped round to the shop next door and bought a beautiful purple dress for Cynthia and a green velvet costume for Tobias.

In the shop Mrs Greensleeves had row upon row of beautiful costumes for all shapes and sizes. If they didn't fit, she could alter the costumes as she was excellent at dressmaking.

Mabble Merlin returned in no time at all, and Cynthia and Tobias couldn't wait to put their costumes on. Mabble Merlin gave them the outfits and they went upstairs to room 103 to change. The room they had was huge and luxurious, with an en-suite bathroom. They were so glad that they didn't have to stay at the Partridge in a Pear Tree, as they were sure they would end up with bed fleas.

From their room window Cynthia and Tobias could see Hampton Court and men on horseback. There seemed to be a lot of activity. People were running about as though something was about to happen. Cynthia wondered what all the commotion was about, and she decided to use the communicator to call headquarters.

She pressed the communicator call button and a voice immediately answered: "Hi. This is Galaxy Zeta, at your service. How can I help you today?"

"Hi, it's Cindy Chimes. I have just a few questions about what is happening outside Hampton Court – and, by the way, what month is it?"

"To answer your question, Cindy, it's January and it's almost time for the wedding of Anne Boleyn and King Henry VIII."

"Oh, my word!" said Cynthia, feeling so excited. "Thank you, Galaxy, for that information."

"I am pleased to inform you, Cindy. Have a nice day," Galaxy replied, and the communicator device fell silent.

Cynthia noticed there was a button to press to bring up a picture of the person she was talking to. She wondered what Galaxy Zeta looked like and where she was from. She hoped she and Tobias would get an invitation to the wedding, and she wondered if it could possibly be arranged. She decided to use the communicator to call headquarters again.

She pressed the communicator button and a voice immediately answered: "Hi. This is Quasar Moon, at your service. How can I help you, Cindy?"

"Oh, hello, Quasar. I was just wondering if we could somehow be invited to King Henry VIII's wedding?"

"Of course you can." Quasar replied. "We'll get you an invitation – we will pass the details on to you in due course. Have a nice day, Cindy."

"So do we have an invitation to the wedding?" asked Tobias.

"We will get the details soon," Cynthia told him. "I feel so excited about going to the wedding – especially if we get to meet King Henry and go inside Hampton Court."

Room 103 was really lovely, and Cynthia and Tobias were so glad they had such luxury comforts in the room, like a hair dryer and a kettle and hot running water. They wondered what someone from the Tudor court would think of what they had. They really wanted to be able to show someone from the Tudor court what modern plumbing and electric circuits could do. Mabble Merlin had advised them to be discreet and not tell anyone, but Cynthia wasn't very good at keeping a secret.

Cynthia and Tobias decided to just relax, so they called room service and ordered some food. A few minutes later there was a knock at the door. Room service had arrived.

"I am Solar Ray and I have brought your food and drinks," came a voice from outside.

Cynthia opened the door and a very lovely lady stood at the door wearing a jumpsuit. She had blonde pageboy hair. Cynthia thought the lady looked very similar to herself.

The lady handed Cynthia a silver tray containing lots of little dishes instead of one large dish. They had ordered an array of Chinese food, and it was certainly cooked nicely. They didn't want to miss out on having food they really enjoyed. They also had a drink each, and this time they were rainbow-coloured.

Included on the tray was a can of spray, which could be used to decontaminate food if there was bacteria on it.

Cynthia and Tobias enjoyed their Chinese food and drinks, and then they decided to get dressed and go to the Partridge in a Pear Tree.

Room 103 was furnished with a four-poster bed and the walls were panelled. It wasn't original sixteenth-century oak, but it looked like it. There was also a bookcase, and they noticed that a book was sticking out from one of the bookshelves. Tobias pushed the book back in, and suddenly the whole room changed. It was transformed into a very futuristic room with reclining chairs and a marble floor. There were crystal lights and fibre-optics lamps and a bed that was named 'The Dreamer' (that is, it was enclosed like a cocoon, and when you went to bed soft music played and lulled you to sleep).

Cynthia and Tobias certainly realised they were in a very big adventure. Their room was incredible. They could either choose to have the Tudor-style room with a Tudor-style luxury bed, or they could have the cocoon-like Dreamer and the fibre-optics lamps and the plasma-screen television, which filled one wall and made them feel as though they were at the cinema.

Suddenly there was a knock at the door and Tobias opened it.

"I've got an invitation to the wedding for the both of you," said Solar Ray, and she handed Tobias a scroll of paper.

Tobias found it difficult to believe that Solar Ray was from another galaxy, and he felt like asking her, but she gave him the scroll and then disappeared along the corridor. He didn't actually see where she went; she just vanished, and he wondered if she had beamed herself up to some sort of space station.

He wondered if it was really 1533 or if it was just like a huge Hollywood stage set. He thought it could be just a huge joke, but he made up his mind to take a lot of photographs of everything he saw, so that when he got back to London in

the year 2010 (the year he'd come from) he would have a portfolio of evidence. After all, he was on a working holiday and he hoped to be able to make a good living from his photographic portfolio. Similarly Cynthia had made up her mind to keep busy, drawing and painting everything. She decided that when she got back to the year 2010 she'd go to the same spots and compare her landscape pictures with what she saw. She sometimes wondered if the whole thing was a dream or a very long hallucination. Things were very bizarre, and she was sure that they would get a lot more bizarre, but she was enjoying the trip.

Cynthia and Tobias thought they were being very well looked after by the strange staff of the Magical Mystery Tours Corporation (working for us, working for you), and they wondered how many staff were working on the trip. They had already met Quantum Phoenix and Solar Ray and Quasar Moon, and they were all most helpful. They looked just as they imagined people of the future would look.

Cynthia was so impressed with the hotel-type room.

"It's above and beyond expectations," she said. "It certainly is beyond expectations," said Tobias. "It's like something from science fiction."

"Well, I have read about people disappearing in the Bermuda Triangle, and sometimes boats and planes disappear too. Possibly they go to the past, just like we have. We may have to stay here in the year 1533 for ever," said Cynthia.

Then Tobias said, "In the *London Times* there was an article about a place in Liverpool – it was Bond Street, just near Lime Street – where people have been walking along the street and suddenly they have found themselves back in the 1960s or 1970s. According to the article, many people have had this experience."

"Well," said Cynthia, "we've just gone a little further back than they have – to the year 1533 – and we got here by taking a trip in a magical musty old shop."

Suddenly there was a knock on their hotel door – room service was there again.

"Who's going to open the door this time?" said Tobias.

"I'll get the door," piped up Cynthia.

She opened the door with a flourish.

"Hi. It's Quark Lunar, at your service. Would you like some refreshments?"

"I would love some doughnuts," said Cynthia.

"And fresh orange juice," called Tobias.

"Anything else?" asked Quark Lunar.

"Well, actually I'd like some perfume," said Cynthia.

"And I would like some aftershave or fragrance – something from Tudor times if possible," called Tobias from the bathroom.

"OK," said Quark. "I will get you these things and be back in a few minutes."

Then Quark Lunar trundled off along the corridor and vanished.

Cynthia had asked for some perfume as she hadn't brought any with her.

As well as the clothes Mabble Merlin had bought from Mrs Greensleeves, there were other outfits and accessories in the wardrobes and drawers, so they had plenty of choice.

Cynthia wondered where Quark Lunar would get the perfume. She also wondered if it would be some sixteenth-century perfume smelling like lavender or pigswill.

Quark Lunar was very slim and handsome. He had long dark hair parted in the middle. He wore a white tunic and trousers and sandals. In fact, he was dressed like someone from India except that he was wearing make-up and nail varnish, and glitter in his hair. Cynthia thought the glitter looks like cosmic dust. She thought she would like to take home some of the glitter and start a fashion trend. It looked like a kind of hair gel with coloured glitter in it. She thought she'd like gold glitter, or silver glitter, or maybe pink glitter, or purple glitter . . .

172

Quark wore a wristwatch communicator, but it was slightly different from Cynthia's. His beeped and made strange noises, and she noticed that he glanced at it from time to time. She decided that someone else requiring room service was possibly giving him a call.

Cynthia thought Quark and the other room-service attendants seemed ultra-relaxed.

Tobias came out of the bathroom. He'd had a power shower, and he was wrapped in a dark blue fluffy bathrobe with his name embroidered on it.

There was a knock at the door and Cynthia swung around to answer the door.

Quark was standing there with a gold tea tray, and it looked like there was a map of the stars on it. There was also a large jug of fresh orange juice and an assortment of doughnuts (jam, vanilla, chocolate, custard and orange) and they were all different shapes. They looked delicious.

Quark put down the tray and handed Cynthia the perfume and aftershave.

"Thank you, Quark," she said.

"Do call again if you need anything," said Quark, and as he whizzed off along the corridor his wristwatch communicator was beeping.

Cynthia quickly opened her perfume, which was called Tudor Dance; and Tobias opened his aftershave, which was called Tudor Soul.

Cynthia sprayed her perfume on, and it certainly didn't smell like pigswill. In fact, it made her feel like dancing. Tobias sprayed on his aftershave, and he immediately felt like a Tudor gentleman of 1533.

Cynthia started to swirl around the hotel room, dancing and singing, but then she realised she didn't know any Tudor dances.

"We don't know any of the Tudor dances, Toby," she said.

"Oh, I'm sure we can call room service and ask Quark to

come and teach us some. If he doesn't know any, I'm sure one of the other 'spacers' will be well versed in Tudor dancing."

At that moment there was another knock at the door, and this time Tobias answered it.

"Is there anything else we can help you with?" asked Quark Lunar.

"As a matter of fact, there is. We don't know any of the Tudor dances and we don't know much about the customs of Tudor times. Is there anyone that could help with that?" asked Tobias.

"Yes," said Quark Lunar, "we have Pulsar Nova. He knows all the Tudor customs and all the dances. He's an historian – a 'spacer' historian."

"Excellent!" said Tobias.

"In fact, Pulsar Nova will be your tour guide. He'll show you around. He has satellite navigation on his wristwatch communicator, so you won't get lost."

"Excellent! Thank you for that, Quark."

"Always at your service, Toby," said Quark, and he ran off along the corridor as if there was no time to lose.

A few minutes later Pulsar Nova knocked on the door of Room 103. He was dressed in Tudor costume, so he looked just like a Tudor gentleman of 1533. He had long dark hair and he had a hint of silver glitter in his hair. He was very slim and handsome. He wore a scarlet-coloured suit with a huge feather in his scarlet velvet cap.

"Hi. I'm Pulsar Nova, at your service. Good morrow, lady and gentleman. 'Tis so good to see you both. I am, of course, your very good tour guide."

"Very good to see you," said Cynthia.

"Pleased to meet you," said Tobias.

"I'll be showing you around 1533 London, and we'll be meeting King Henry VIII and Anne Boleyn."

An Evening Out in Tudor London

"Shall we dilly-dally no more? Let's go," piped up Pulsar.

The three of them walked along the corridor until they came to a space-age-looking elevator. Cynthia, Tobias and Pulsar got into the elevator, Pulsar pressed a button and the elevator whizzed downwards. When it came to a halt, they stepped out into a wide corridor and then went through a door and came out in a small courtyard with a few trees and wooden benches. It looked like a typical Tudor courtyard. Then they all walked out of the courtyard and out into the Tudor night.

As they walked along the street, everyone was friendly and said "Hello" and "Good morrow". They all seemed to think Cynthia, Tobias and Pulsar belonged there in Tudor London.

Pulsar looked very handsome and he had a lovely smile. He seemed to know his way along the streets. The ladies seemed to like Pulsar; they all smiled and said hello.

The little cobbled streets looked so quaint – there was a blacksmith's shop and a cobbler's shop and a butcher's shop with lots of pheasants and rabbits hanging in the window.

The streets were a little bit smelly, but there were no tin cans rolling in the gutters and no newspapers. On the other hand, there were a great many trees – in fact they had to go in and out of the trees. They had to keep ducking and diving.

The three of them walked for a while along the street, until at last they came to Hampton Court. It looked very splendid. It was so large. Tobias wanted to take some photographs of it, so he got his camera out of his satchel and took several pictures. He also took several of Cynthia and Pulsar Nova, and then he asked Pulsar to take some photographs of him with Cynthia, standing in front of Hampton Court.

Cynthia took out a sketch pad and made a few sketches. She was quite pleased with them, and she thought she might spend more time the next day working them up into a painting.

Pulsar did something with his wristwatch communicator, which also seemed to be taking photographs.

Tobias took a few pictures of the trees, as they were huge, very impressive oak trees. He also took photographs of the street and the butcher's shop and the pheasants and rabbits hanging in the window.

Then they made their way to the Partridge in a Pear Tree. Inside, there was a wooden floor covered with sawdust. The parlour was furnished with hand-carved furniture. They thought it looked rather cool. A large open fire was burning bright. A group of patrons dressed in the finest clothes sat huddled together talking, with large pewter jugs of ale on the table in front of them.

Cynthia, Tobias and Pulsar decided to have a tankard of cider each.

Everyone was so friendly to them – very chatty. No one seemed to realise that they had just arrived by time travel in the Musty Old Magical Curiosity Shop.

Bartholomew Mead brought the cider to the table in pewter tankards. His wife, Eleanor Mead, poured out the cider for them.

"Thank you," said Pulsar Nova.

Tobias tasted the cider.

"It tastes very good," he said.

"It's from our own apple orchard," said Eleanor, seeming very pleased.

She handed the three of them a bread bun each with their drinks. They looked as though they had just been baked, and there was a lovely smell of freshly baked bread.

"We're on holiday," said Cynthia.

"Oh, where are you staying?" asked Eleanor.

"We're staying at a tavern not far from here," piped up Pulsar.

"Which one is that?" asked Eleanor.

"It's the Half Moon Tavern in Orchard Court," piped up Pulsar Nova.

Cynthia and Tobias were so glad that Pulsar was with them, because they really wouldn't have known what to say to Eleanor's questions.

"Oh, yes," said Eleanor. "That's a lovely little tavern."

"Yes, it is," said Pulsar Nova.

"Well, I do hope you enjoy your holiday," said Eleanor.

The Partridge in a Pear Tree wasn't very crowded, and the time-travellers were just enjoying the peaceful atmosphere when suddenly in walked a very loud, boisterous group of people. They were musicians from Hampton Court. There were forty of them. They had come to enjoy a few drinks in the tavern and play their music and sing the songs of the day. They were all excellent musicians, and King Henry had chosen them himself. Their names were:

Eric Goldstein	Angelo Cello
Steve Trimble	Stanley Tunes
Hugh Moon	Stephanie Blues
Jaxon Domino	Rebecca Choir
Kirsty Silvano	Dennis Wardrop
Paul Keys	Julia Concerto

Sarah Quaver	Mary Waltz
Gareth Bows	Edith Starstruck
James Cruickshank	Imogen Snowball
Alison Songbird	Guy Gold
Lucas Lyrics	Marcus Bachelor
Carolyn Velvet	Wilfred Accordion
Valery Wompra	Eddie Tambourine
Max Millions	Martin O'Leary
Hildegard Fiddle	Janey Breeze
Cedric Cold	Horace Chutney
Gina Lorenzo	Bridgette Lacey
Joshua Buddleia	Hazel Queen
Kaye Noteby	Percy Plumstone
Gerald Bolshy	Victoria English.

The tavern was now full to the brim. Twelve of the musicians sat around the table where Cynthia, Tobias and Pulsar sat. These musicians were:

Steve Trimble	Lucas Lyrics
Hugh Moon	Carolyn Velvet
Jaxon Domino	Gina Lorenzo
Paul Keys	Kaye Noteby
Sarah Quaver	Guy Gold
Gareth Bows	Janey Breeze

The musicians asked Cynthia, Tobias and Pulsar to join in with the singing as the musicians played their instruments and sang. Hugh Moon noticed that Cynthia had an unusual accent, and he asked her where she was from.

"We're from across the water – New York, actually."

"I've never heard of New York, but I haven't actually been abroad," said Hugh.

Pulsar was talking to Sarah Quaver, and Tobias was talking to Steve Trimble.

The words of the songs were, in some cases, very simple, and Cynthia and Tobias felt confident enough to sing along loudly in their New York accents.

"Bravo! Bravo!" piped up Jaxon Domino.

Of course Pulsar sang very well indeed.

Lucas Lyrics handed Cynthia, Tobias and Pulsar a tambourine each, to really get into the swing, and Pulsar fetched several scrolls of music from out of his satchel and handed them to Cynthia and Tobias so that they could keep up with the songs. They were glad Pulsar was there to help out. Largely thanks to him they were able to enjoy the evening at the Partridge in a Pear Tree.

Guy Gold, who played the flute, asked Pulsar where he was from. Pulsar brought out a star map to show Guy Gold, but Guy thought it was hilarious. He thought Pulsar was having a joke.

"You're fooling about!" he said.

"Where are you staying?" asked Gina Lorenzo.

"We're staying at the Half Moon Tavern in Orchard Court."

"Oh, that's strange – some of our musicians are staying there. We sometimes play at the Half Moon Tavern."

"Excellent!" said Pulsar. "We must meet up there one night."

"Why not?" said Gina Lorenzo.

They all had some more cider and hot bread buns, which had just been baked, and they all had a very enjoyable evening. They were glad they didn't have far to walk back to their room above the Musty Old Magical Curiosity Shop as they were so tired.

They thought it so funny when Pulsar got out the star map to show the musicians where Cygnus Xi was; all the musicians seemed to have a great sense of humour.

Dance Lessons

Next morning when Cynthia and Tobias woke up it wasn't long before there was a knock on the door. It was room service. They wondered if room service ever stopped for five minutes; they had to admit it was great service.

Tobias pulled on his dressing gown and answered the door. There was a new 'spacer' standing there.

"Hi. I'm Delta Zenith. What would you like for breakfast?"

"We'd like fresh pineapple juice, a cup of tea each and a fried breakfast – eggs, sausages, tomatoes, mushrooms and fried bread," said Tobias.

"That's fine. We'll have that ready in just a few minutes."

Delta Zenith whizzed off along the corridor, just like the others.

It wasn't long before she was back with a large gold tray with a star map engraved on it. She brought the fresh pineapple juice, two cups of tea and a lovely-looking fried breakfast. She also had a purple vase with a bunch of lilac, freesias, pansies and chrysanthemums. It was lovely of Delta to think of such a thing.

Cynthia looked out of the little square leaded windows, and she noticed a lot of commotion outside Hampton Court, where preparations were under way for the wedding of King Henry VIII and Anne Boleyn. She decided she wanted to purchase something as a wedding present, so she used the communicator to call the Magical Mystery Tours headquarters to see if they could help.

"Hi. It's Pulsar Nova. How can I help you, Cindy?"

"Hi, Pulsar," said Cynthia. "Toby and I would love to purchase a wedding gift for King Henry VIII and Anne Boleyn; as it wouldn't be right to go to the wedding without a gift. By the way, when exactly is the wedding?"

"The wedding is on the 25th of January in Hampton Court Palace — just a few days' time. I will ask Captain Mabble Merlin if he will let you choose a wedding gift from the shop. I'm sure he will have something suitable."

"OK, Pulsar, that's great! Speak to you later," said Cynthia.

Cynthia and Tobias had decided to stick with the futuristic room, with its marble floor, soft blue lights and the futuristic bed – 'The Dreamer'. The room seemed much bigger than it did with Tudor furnishings.

Suddenly there was a knock at the door. It was room service.

Tobias answered the door and Pulsar Nova and Stellar Fusion came into the room. Stellar Fusion was going to teach them how to do Tudor dances. She was a skilled dancer. She wore a lime-green leotard, a pink tutu and lime-green dance shoes. She had her hair arranged in three little buns, she wore flowers in her hair, and she had butterfly designs painted on the side of her face. She looked very cosmic. She seemed to glide across the floor when she walked. She was very happy to show Cynthia and Tobias how Tudor dances were performed, and it wasn't too difficult for them to learn the routines. One of the dances was a very silly dance; it was so funny that Cynthia and Tobias couldn't stop laughing. It was called the Dance of the Pink Flamingos. You had to turn your head to one side and shuffle along on tiptoes and then turn your head to the other side and shuffle the other way on tiptoes. They couldn't imagine King Henry doing this dance, but Stellar Fusion said it was the wedding dance.

At Mrs Greensleeves' Shop

Pulsar decided to take Cynthia and Tobias into Mrs Greensleeves' dressmaker's shop. Pulsar knew that Anne Boleyn would be in the shop having her wedding dress fitted, and it was a good opportunity for them to meet her.

Pulsar took them into the dressmaker's, which was full of lovely clothes just suitable for the wedding of a king. Anne Boleyn was already there. She spun round and Cynthia and Tobias were face-to-face with her. She was very pretty and charming. They couldn't understand why King Henry would ever want to chop her head off. Cynthia and Tobias didn't really know what to say to her, but Pulsar stepped forward and introduced himself.

"Hi. I'm Pulsar," he said. "We have got an invitation to your wedding on Saturday, and we're really looking forward to it."

"I'm very pleased you're able to come," said Anne Boleyn. "I do hope the three of you enjoy your day."

Pulsar wanted to tell Anne Boleyn he had a plan to save her from having her head chopped off, but he just replied, "I really hope you have a lovely wedding day."

Mabble Merlin had decided to try to save her. He had already thought of a plan to replace the real Anne Boleyn with a clone so that she could be saved.

Mabble Merlin didn't want to spoil the wedding by

telling Anne Boleyn that she wasn't going to last very long as the wife of King Henry VIII, so he had decided to let her enjoy the wedding. After all, it was going to be a very good wedding.

The Wedding of Henry VIII and Anne Boleyn

When Cynthia and Tobias woke up on the morning of the wedding, they felt so excited. It was a fairly cold day, yet the sky was very blue and little fluffy clouds were floating by. They were sure they were going to enjoy the day.

They had decided to give King Henry and Anne Boleyn a dressing mirror each as a wedding gift; and Cynthia also wanted to give them something extra, so she purchased a gold-coloured silk quilt, handmade in China, using silk from more than 1,000 silkworms. It was very eye-catching, and there were matching gold silk sheets and a matching bolster. Bolsters are long tube-like pillows. They aren't very comfortable and they don't look comfortable. Cynthia would have preferred to give them goose-down-filled duvets and pillows, but, believe it or not, in 1533 square feather pillows hadn't been invented, and neither had duvets.

However, the full-length dressing mirror might be useful: when King Henry made up his mind to behead her, Anne Boleyn might have to escape through the mirror.

Cynthia and Tobias got dressed for the wedding. They wore the outfits Mabble Merlin had bought from Mrs Greensleeves. They looked perfect.

There was a knock on the door; Pulsar and Stellar Fusion had arrived. Pulsar was wearing a midnight-blue velvet outfit with a very large velvet hat and a feather. Stellar wore a purple dress with a silver floral pattern.

They all felt very Tudor, but Tobias also had his satchel with his camera inside. Come what may, he was determined to take some photographs. He thought that once the wedding started, and everyone had had a few drinks, nobody would notice him taking a few photographs. King Henry was sure to keep the punch flowing and Bartholomew and Eleanor Mead would be there with barrels of cider from their apple orchard. Pulsar Nova and Stellar Fusion were intending to take photographs of the wedding with their wristwatch communicators, which took perfect digital photographs.

They didn't have far to walk to Hampton Court. It was so amazing to see it in Tudor times, not long after it had been built. King Henry looked amazing with his copper-coloured hair and sparkly blue eyes. He was very boisterous and laughed all the time, and he patted his guests on the back with his hard shovel-like hands. If he hadn't been a king, he should have been a builder, or an architect.

Cynthia and Tobias got the giggles. When King Henry was laughing they were laughing. They felt a bit nervous about being there, but Pulsar and Stellar were as cool as cucumbers or cooler. They didn't seem nervous at all.

At the wedding service there was a hushed silence. Everyone seemed to take it very seriously. King Henry looked fabulous in his wedding suit, with a rich red-and-gold tapestry design and a huge hat with a feather in it. Anne Boleyn had a beautiful golden wedding dress, with lots of layers of silk and lace, and a gold lace wedding veil, and she had her dark hair piled up high on her head.

'It could be a New York celebrity wedding,' thought Cynthia. She was glad she didn't laugh or cough or get the giggles.

When the service was over, there was a banquet on the longest tables you ever saw. The guests were so busy looking at King Henry and Anne Boleyn that they didn't drink or eat very much, but King Henry had a very good appetite. He ate with gusto, as though he was famished. He tucked in to huge chicken legs – in fact, he had about ten of them piled on a pewter plate in front of him. Anne Boleyn also had a lot to eat, but she ate more delicately, wiping her mouth with a napkin and sipping wine between mouthfuls.

Cynthia was staring over at the King maybe a little too much, and before long he noticed her and gave her a little smile; but then he went straight back to a very large chicken leg – or possibly it was a turkey leg. Cynthia couldn't be sure as she was a long way across the room.

Then it was time for a speech from King Henry. He stood up and spoke in a very loud, commanding voice. He said he was glad everyone had come and he remarked on how lovely the food and wine was. He particularly mentioned Bartholomew Mead for the excellent cider and Mrs Greensleeves for making the wedding outfits. He also thanked his musicians for the music during the wedding ceremony, and he named every one of them. He seemed to have an excellent memory for names. The baker who had moved to Tintagel had come back to London especially to make the pies and the cakes, including the very large wedding cake (which was in the shape of Hampton Court, with figures of King Henry and Anne Boleyn holding hands on top of it).

The King went on to say how beautiful Anne Boleyn looked, and he said there was no one in the world like her. "Her pretty head is just perfect," he said. "She has beauty, wit and poise, and she could charm the birds out of the trees." Then he said he'd written a song for her called 'Lady Golden Sleeves'.

With that, the musicians began to play and the choir began to sing:

LADY GOLDEN SLEEVES

Lady Golden Sleeves is my joy,
My only joy, one true joy,
There's no one in the world
That brings me so much joy.
My one and only joy,
With her long dark hair,
Her misty eyes,
Her ruby lips like crimson skies!
I will devote my love to her
As she's my only one true joy,
My only joy,
My one and only joy.

She's my happiness,
My sweet caress.
She melted my heart
One summer's day,
And all I could say
Was "You are my joy,
My one and only joy,
My one true joy.
My only joy, my only joy."
And she's my Lady Golden Sleeves,
Sweeter than a summer's breeze –
She gives me so much joy!

King Henry VIII had written the words himself and he had written the music with the help of his twelve foremost musicians.

After this serenade the dancing began, while all forty musicians played their music.

Cynthia and Tobias thought it was an excellent wedding. They each had a little tear in their eye to think that before

long the King would want to behead his new bride, so they were pleased that Mabble Merlin had a plan to save her from getting her head chopped off. Nevertheless, whatever the future might hold, their wedding day was just a lovely, joyful occasion – exactly how King Henry had described it.

Cynthia and Tobias wondered what on earth would go wrong to make him want to do such a ghastly thing to Anne Boleyn. She was so sweet. It didn't seem possible that she could make him so mad. She did, though, have one hobby he didn't like very much, and that was that she liked to write a lot. She would even write in the very middle of the night, and King Henry didn't think this was very appropriate now that they were married. It was not surprising if now and then he put his foot down and shouted, "That's enough, Anne Boleyn! Please put that feather pen down."

In 1533 there were only feather pens, and sometimes the ink got spilt and it would ruin clothes if it got on them. Writing with a feather pen (a quill, as it was named) wasn't very easy, but Anne Boleyn's writing was very elegant. She was writing a book about religion, and she intended to continue working on it after she was married. Before the wedding King Henry didn't realise it would become a problem. He was full of joy, and had eyes only for his new queen, Anne Boleyn.

The wedding was in full swing and everyone was in high spirits. They ate more food, drank more punch, drank more wine, drank more cider and drank more ale, and most of them were getting very merry.

Cynthia and Tobias and Pulsar and Stellar got up to do the dances they had all learnt to do so perfectly, and they danced around the room changing partners and thoroughly enjoying themselves. The ladies seem to love Pulsar, and the gentlemen loved Stellar. They danced and danced until they forgot where they were. Everyone was most charming.

Suddenly the music and dancing stopped and King Henry summoned them to his table. He had noticed that they danced excellently, and he had noticed Pulsar getting all the attention from the ladies and Stellar getting all the attention from the gentlemen, and Cynthia had been staring at him whilst he was eating, so he was a bit curious to know who they were. He had assumed they were from across the water, like his first wife, who was Spanish.

His first wife was Catherine of Aragon, and he married her on 11 June 1509 in Greyfriars Church. Catherine was a Spanish princess. Henry divorced her because he wanted a son. She had been married to his brother Arthur, but Arthur had died.

"Where are you both from? I can tell your accent is different," he asked Cynthia and Tobias.

"We are from across the water," said Cynthia.

"New York, actually, King Henry," said Tobias.

"And what are your names?"

They all introduced themselves, and then King Henry said, "Pulsar? That's a very unusual name! And Stellar Fusion? That's a very interesting name! Where are you both from?"

"We're from Cygnus Xi. It's a wormhole," piped up Pulsar.

"Oh, I get your meaning," said King Henry, and he laughed very loudly. "Some places around here are wormholes – or I could use a stronger word, but I won't say it in front of the ladies. I also call them ratholes."

Cynthia and Tobias laughed, and the others laughed too.

"Thank you very much for the wedding gift," said King Henry as he shook Tobias's hand. "And thank you very much for your gift, Stellar and Pulsar."

They had given King Henry a gold tray inlaid with gemstones and engraved with constellations. Cygnus Xi was one of the stars engraved on it.

King Henry asked what it was.

"It's a map of the stars."

"I will take a look at that, but I admit I don't know much about the heavens. I leave that to the court astrologer, Leo Starchase, but I may take it up as a hobby."

Stellar had also given him and Anne Boleyn matching goblets with gemstones and star maps on them – also featuring Cygnus Xi (the famous wormhole).

King Henry had no idea Pulsar meant he came from another galaxy. He thought he was saying the place he came from was a fleapit. In 1533 there were a lot of fleas about, and some places had more than others. There were a lot of rats too, and the King had to employ ten rats-catchers at Hampton Court alone. Even so, the odd rat still found its way in; if he saw it, he'd hit it over the head with a frying pan, or anything else he could lay his hands on at the time.

Anne Boleyn asked Cynthia where they had their clothes made, and she said they were made in Mrs Greensleeves' shop. Anne Boleyn said they were the best designs she'd ever seen. There were slight differences to the normal couture of the day, especially in the outfits of Pulsar and Stellar, and Mrs Greensleeves used only the best materials, which cost a lot of money. The rose-quartz necklace Cynthia wore was the best Anne Boleyn had seen, she said, and Cynthia said she would get her one like it. King Henry wanted an outfit like the one Pulsar was wearing. He liked something a little bit unusual to wear; he liked to stand out in a crowd.

"This isn't my first marriage," he piped up to Cynthia.

"Oh, I know, King Henry!"

"Oh?" said King Henry.

"Well, Mrs Greensleeves told us," piped up Pulsar.

Tobias felt like saying, "And it won't be your last!" but he said nothing.

"Good Lord, I shouldn't keep on getting married!" cried King Henry. "It costs too much." Then he laughed and the others all joined in.

Cynthia felt like saying, "Well, actually you'll have Anne Boleyn's head chopped off on May the 19th 1536 at the Tower of London. Then you'll get married to wife number three, Jane Seymour, on May the 20th 1536 in York Place, and that marriage will end on October the 27th 1537. Then you'll marry wife number four, Anne of Cleves, on January the 6th 1540. That marriage will end in 1540." (Anne of Cleves was not to King Henry's liking: she had a derrière as big as Flanders.) "Then you'll marry wife number five, Catherine Howard, on July the 28th 1540, and that marriage will end on February the 13th 1542 – head chopped off. Wife number six, Catherine Parr, will marry you on July the 12th 1543 at Hampton Court. That marriage will end in 1547 when you pop your clogs."

King Henry would get married six times in total, but Cynthia wisely decided to say nothing about any of this.

King Henry had a great sense of humour despite his many faults.

Then the musicians started up again and they went back for some more dancing. They were all a bit merry with the punch and cider and wine, so Tobias decided to take photographs. Pulsar had taken some pictures of the wedding service, and Tobias had also managed to take a few while no one was looking. Now there were so many people dancing and laughing and eating and drinking that no one took any notice of what Tobias was up to. Cynthia made a few sketches of things, and Pulsar and Stellar took hundreds of digital photographs with their wristwatch communicators. Copies of these pictures would eventually be given to Cynthia and Tobias for their portfolios, and Cynthia was able to make paintings from the best ones.

As all the guests were very merry, Tobias decided to ask the musicians to play a few songs from his own time. He quickly wrote out the music for a few songs from the

1960s and 1970s and presented them to the musicians, who agreed to give them a go.

When the wedding guests heard this music they thought it was a bit strange at first, but Cynthia and Tobias started dancing. They did the twist, and then they started to dance freestyle, just moving all over the floor and freaking out. All the guests thought it was fantastic and they all took to the floor, dancing wildly.

Pulsar and Stellar captured all the guests on their wristwatch communicators as they freaked out and danced wildly.

They too thought the music was fantastic.

Then Pulsar and Stellar persuaded the musicians to play their kind of music from Cygnus Xi. It was weird space-age-type music, and Pulsar did some sort of moonwalk. He pressed a button on his wristwatch communicator and some sort of disco spotlight came upon him. First it was orange, then it was blue, then white, then gold, then silver. His wristwatch communicator added a groovy beat to the music the musicians were playing, and then Stellar started to dance some sort of cosmic dance. As she danced she pressed a button on her wristwatch communicator and it looked like silver rain was falling on her – it also added a strobe-lighting effect. Then she pressed another button and smoke appeared.

The wedding guests were mesmerised. They had never seen anything like it in their lives. They were all clapping, and some were shouting, "Bravo! Bravo!"

King Henry and Anne Boleyn thought these guests were amazing. They thought maybe New York was a very fine place, and maybe Cygnus Xi was even more amazing.

In the end it had turned out to be a very joyous and amazing wedding; King Henry and Anne Boleyn and the wedding guests would never ever forget it.

Anne Boleyn Is Cloned

After the wedding, Cynthia and Tobias stayed for a while in 1533. In fact, they were there for months. They learnt to horse-ride, and Tobias managed to take hundreds of photographs of the architecture and the streets and people. Cynthia painted hundreds of pictures. They met lots of people and they visited the Half Moon Tavern. They even had picnics in the woods near Hampton Court. However, they knew that even though Anne Boleyn was very happy during this time, someone would have to tell her that one day her husband would want to have her head chopped off, so she would have to be cloned so that she could be saved.

Mabble Merlin decided she would have to visit the Musty Old Magical Curiosity Shop and he would have to tell her.

Henry's birthday was on 24 June, and when Anne Boleyn was thinking about buying a birthday present she noticed the Musty Old Magical Curiosity Shop. She was very happy to see such a nice little shop, and she went inside to get something special.

Mabble Merlin decided to show her a crystal ball so she could see herself getting her head chopped off. He knew she wouldn't like it, and possibly she would sob her eyes out, but he hoped she would realise he was trying to help her.

Anne Boleyn hadn't made up her mind what she would buy for a king that had everything. She thought she might buy him a hat or possibly some jewellery, or both.

Mabble Merlin suddenly piped up: "How can I help you, Queen Anne Boleyn?"

"Well, I have come in to buy King Henry a birthday present. It will be his birthday soon."

Mabble Merlin said, "Can I show you something that is very special? It can foretell the future, and it never lies."

Anne Boleyn said, "Why, yes, I would love to see something that foretells the future."

Mabble Merlin took out the crystal ball, and straight away it started to cloud over. There was a huge clap of thunder (or it sounded like thunder) and Anne Boleyn jumped. She just didn't know what to think, or what she was going to see. Suddenly the crystal ball cleared and she saw, as clear as day, a horrible scene. It looked as though she was getting her head chopped off. She screamed so loudly Mabble Merlin thought everything in the shop would jump. Then she started to sob and sob and sob and sob.

Mabble Merlin called Pulsar and Stellar, and he called for Cynthia and Tobias, and they all came to the shop immediately.

Mabble Merlin gave Anne Boleyn a cup of tea, and some tissues to dry her eyes. Cynthia put her arm around her.

"Don't worry, Anne Boleyn," she said. "We have a plan – a very good plan."

Then Mabble Merlin told Anne Boleyn what he planned to do: he would replace her with a clone, and she, the real Anne Boleyn, could stay out of harm's way in the accommodation above the shop while the Anne Boleyn clone would go and have her head chopped off in her place. He pointed out to her that King Henry wouldn't know the difference, and she could have a great laugh about that.

Eventually Anne Boleyn calmed down. When Mabble Merlin explained what a clone was, she thought the plan was excellent, and she thanked him for helping her. She couldn't believe Mabble Merlin was so nice to her. She bought King Henry a huge hat for his birthday and a gold necklace engraved with her name: Anne Boleyn. It turned out to be the last gift he ever received from her.

Pulsar and Stellar said the twelve musicians of King Henry's court were so fantastic that they wanted to take them with them when they all left 1533 with the real Anne Boleyn. Mabble Merlin agreed because he knew at least four of the musicians were also due to get their heads chopped off. King Henry could search high and low for them, but he'd never find them!

Mabble Merlin had to get down to work on Anne Boleyn's clone, so he wasted no time. She was taken to the Antimatter Fusion Teleportation Chamber, and she was beamed up to the Magical Mystery Tour headquarters, where the technicians made a clone of her. This didn't take them long, and, when the clone had been completed, into Mabble Merlin's shop walked two identical Anne Boleyns. Cynthia and Tobias couldn't tell the difference, but Pulsar went straight up to the clone and took it out of the shop. He said, "This one can now go back to the court."

Anne Boleyn had already given her clone the birthday present for King Henry, and the clone was at Hampton Court before anyone realised Anne Boleyn was missing. The real Anne Boleyn of course stayed in accommodation above the shop, but Mabble Merlin told her that the mirror in her room at Hampton Court was magical and she could go and come back through the mirror.

She said she might possibly go if King Henry went away to his castle in Kent, and if she felt a bit homesick, but she told Mabble Merlin she expected to enjoy her new life above the shop.

The Four Just Men and the Pie Fight

King Henry was getting rather sick of Anne Boleyn being so perfect. He didn't know she was a clone, which was why she was able to do everything just perfectly, but he knew he was sick to his back teeth of her being so utterly perfect.

One day he wanted to have fun, and to just do something different, so he said to his Four Just Men, who were standing close by, "Let's do something different today. Let's let our hair down."

His Four Just Men were Peter Pumpernickel, who hated to see food going to waste; Terry Barrels, who loved good beer; Ken Wolf, who always wolfed down his food without pausing for breath; and Ronnie Rumble, who was a bit on the huge side but nimble on his feet.

King Henry's Four Just Men always stood close to King Henry. They were just his friends whom he liked to have fun with, and on this day he decided it was time for fun. He told Ken Wolf that he wanted to get 2,000 pies and plenty of beer and just have a pie fight.

"Can you go to the baker's over the road in Orchard Court and get me 2,000 pies?" he said. "We're going to have a pie fight today."

Ken rushed across to the baker's to get the 2,000 pies, but the baker's was no longer in Orchard Court. The baker had moved to Tintagel, and the Musty Old Magical Curiosity Shop was now in its place.

While Ken was wondering what to do next, Cynthia, Tobias and Pulsar came walking along the road, and Ken asked them if they knew where he could get 2,000 pies.

"Well," said Pulsar, "I think we can help you. We can get you 2,000 pies – don't worry about that."

"Oh, thank goodness for that!" said Ken. "I remember now – Hector Spice went to Cornwall, and he opened a shop down in Tintagel called The Cornish Pasty."

Pulsar went into the Musty Old Magical Curiosity Shop and asked Mabble Merlin for 2,000 pies. Mabble Merlin had to send an order through to headquarters to get 2,000 pies, but in a very short time 2,000 pies were beamed down from the headquarters bakery – and they made the best pies ever. The only worry was that King Henry might like the pies so much he wouldn't want to have the pie fight, but there were enough pies to have a pie fight and also to eat some of them. Mabble Merlin hoped the pie fight would cheer King Henry up, because he felt a bit guilty about cloning his wife and he knew the clone was a bit too perfect for the King's liking.

Pulsar helped Ken Wolf to take the 2,000 pies back to Hampton Court.

King Henry thought it was great to see so many pies, and Ken Wolf put them all on the large table in the dining room. Peter Pumpernickel also thought they looked good – good enough to eat. He didn't like to see food going to waste. He was just about to eat one of the pies when King Henry threw one of the pies at him and started the pie fight.

The Four Just Men (Ken Wolf, Peter Pumpernickel, Terry Barrels and Ronnie Rumbles) and King Henry were soon having a great time, throwing the pies at one another. They threw pies for hours and hours.

Anne Boleyn looked in, and the dining room by that time was such a mess. There were pies everywhere. But she just said, "Oh, dear! Oh, dear! I will have to clean all this up later."

King Henry told the Four Just Men that Anne Boleyn was too perfect and that she stayed up all night writing, and when he got up in the morning she was still writing. He said she was so perfect that it was really getting on his nerves.

"She's so perfect; she's too perfect. She's like a clone," King Henry shouted as he threw another pie. The very thought put him in a temper.

Little did he know that Anne Boleyn really was a clone.

Peter Pumpernickel was feeling a bit sick of all the food going to waste, so he decided to lie on the floor and pretend he was too tired to keep throwing pies. Actually every time a pie fell on him he scoffed it, and it was very delicious. Peter had never tasted pies like that before. They were so different! He couldn't stop scoffing them whenever King Henry's back was turned.

"Come on! Get up, Peter, and join in," shouted King Henry, but Peter pretended to be too tired and he continued to scoff the pies behind the others' backs. Sometimes one half of the pie was chicken and one half was rhubarb.

'A delicious sweet and savoury pie!' he thought.

After the pie fight the room was an absolute mess. All the pies were squashed and broken, and the men were covered with splattered pies. By this time they were all so tired, and they all fell asleep on the dining-room floor.

Queen Anne Boleyn's clone came in with one of her ladies-in-waiting, who was named Beth Silks, and they picked all of the pies up off the floor and cleaned the room and carried the Four Just Men and King Henry up to their rooms and put them to bed.

Razzamatazz

King Henry was so sick of Anne Boleyn being so perfect. She was too perfect. When she ironed his clothes, she ironed them perfectly with neat creases. She put the heavy iron on the fire until it was hot, and ironed shirts all night long. She even ironed his leggings.

King Henry didn't like it one little bit, and one day he said to the Four Just Men that he couldn't stand it any longer. He told them he was thinking of chopping her head off.

The Four Just Men thought he was being silly, but the idea was nagging away in Henry's mind. He couldn't sleep some nights, so he went out on his horse, and one night he galloped all the way to York. In York Woods it just so happened that he saw a young lady riding a white horse, and he decided he would talk to her. He found out her name was Jane Seymour.

When he got back to Hampton Court he still couldn't sleep, and he was very tired the next day. He sat in the drawing room with his Four Just Men wondering what to do.

Peter Pumpernickel said, "Shall we have another pie fight, King Henry?"

Henry was so mad and fed up that he said, "Off with you, Pumpernickel," and he gave him such a push that he whizzed along the floor and bounced off the wall. King Henry shouted, "Make yourself scarce, Pumpernickel, or it will be 'off with your head' next!"

The other three men also made themselves scarce, as King Henry was in such a rage.

King Henry stomped across the drawing room and tripped over the rat-catching cat, which was called Razzamatazz, and he said, "Off with your head, you silly fat cat, for getting in my way! Don't you know I'm the King?"

The cat replied, "I am Razzamatazz, the rat-catcher."

King Henry thought he'd had too much of the ale – a new brand named Grog Ale that Bartholomew Mead had brought in for him to taste.

'I've had too much grog and too little sleep,' he told himself. 'Now I'm imagining that cats can talk.'

He had also had too much of Anne Boleyn writing in the night, so he made up his mind that that night he'd get on his horse and gallop all the way to York to see the mysterious Jane Seymour on her white horse.

Suddenly Mog Og woke up. He had been having a bit of a nightmare and in his sleep he'd heard King Henry shouting, "Off with your head, you silly fat cat!" Mog Og thought the King meant him.

Mog Og told Poly Quazar about his strange dream and he asked her what it meant.

Polly Quazar said that in the sixteenth century there was a king called Henry VIII who had a rat-catching cat called Razzamatazz. She said King Henry liked chopping people's heads off, and that probably included cats' heads if they tripped him up.

"Oh, goodness me!" said Mog Og. "I wouldn't like to live in King Henry's court because I'd always be tripping him up."

The Clocks Come Back Home

Milly Paris had attended Tick-Tock School, and she had passed with flying colours. Mog Og went to collect her from Mabble Merlin's shop and brought her back home. He put her on the sofa instead of putting her back in the dusty closet, and the next morning Miles noticed that she was working perfectly. He didn't know how that had come about, but he put her back on the wall. Claudette de Seconds had decided not to come back. She asked to be taken back to the French court, and Mabble Merlin decided that was the best thing to do. She never again went back to the Laugherty household.

All the other clocks were repaired and in even better condition than when they were new. Miles was willing to collect them, but Mabble Merlin said he would deliver them back to their house, and this is what he did.

George Midnight, the grandfather clock, was feeling better than ever; Jasmine Feathersprings felt perfect and had a spring in her step; and Omega Horizon had had a facelift (a bit of a nip and tuck). Omega had her clock face seen to as it was cracked, but now she looked sensational with a slight tint to her face – as if she had a suntan.

The family were very pleased about the clocks returning in pristine condition. Mog Og was so glad they were back – especially his good friend George. He was over the moon, and he was looking forward to enjoying a lovely Christmas. He was so happy that Milly was back on the wall; and now she could tell the time perfectly – she didn't miss a beat. She could tick and tock as well as anyone.

Polly Quazar was also glad to have Milly back on the kitchen wall.

All the clocks knew Claudette de Seconds would be going back to the French court, where she could be pampered, and they were very pleased for her.

The Magical Christmas Fairy

Penelope loved shopping at Christmas time. She decided to buy some new tinsel and bows, a new Christmas tree and a new Christmas fairy for the Christmas tree. The Christmas fairy they had was named Christabella, and she was going to sit on the mantelpiece from now on, as she was sick of sitting on the top of the Christmas tree.

Christabella wore a pretty cream dress with gold feathers on the bottom of the dress and the sleeves, and she had pretty glittery gold wings, blonde curly hair and green eyes. She was very happy to sit on the mantelpiece next to the snowman, who was named Jack Snowball. He was very friendly.

Penelope went shopping in the Bayswater area, and it wasn't long before she came across the Musty Old Magical Curiosity Shop. It was between a decorating shop called Paintbrush Alley and a very nice café called The Six Wise Monkeys Tea and Coffee Shop.

Penelope went into Mabble Merlin's shop, and very soon saw just what she was looking for – a Christmas fairy.

Mabble Merlin said she was named Pumby Ely Fuddles, and Penelope said, "That's a very unusual name for a Christmas fairy."

"Well, she is an unusual Christmas fairy," he replied. "And she will be just perfect for your Christmas tree."

Penelope purchased her, and she was especially pleased because she thought Pumby would be a friend for

Christabella. She looked lovely in her cerise dress, with her long, dark hair, light-blue eyes and silver wings.

Penelope went into the café next door to get a cup of tea and a scone, and as she sat drinking her tea she thought she heard a voice say, "I'm a magical Christmas fairy with special powers." But Penelope decided she had imagined it.

She looked at the drawing of the six wise monkeys on the coffee-shop sign. There were three monkeys standing in a row. These said, "See no evil," "Speak no evil" and "Hear no evil." Two monkeys stood on their shoulders, and they said, "Think no evil" and "Feel no evil." And there was one monkey standing on the shoulders of those two, and this one said, "Dream no evil."

They were the Happy Tumbling Monkeys.

Penelope thought the tea was really nice and the scone was delicious. She felt sure it was going to be a great Christmas.

The Chocolate Advent Clock

It was the festive season, Christmas time, and the Christmas lights had been switched on in London. Everyone just thought, 'Wow!' Everything just sparkled with colour and life.

The Laugherty family decided to go Christmas shopping in the Bayswater area. They all thought that Christmas in London was magical, with the Christmas lights and the atmosphere and the smell of Christmas wafting through the air.

Because Christmas is a magical time, the Musty Old Magical Curiosity Shop had appeared dramatically once again. It was now squashed between an Indian restaurant called The Indian Spice Experience and a sweet shop called Sweet As Candy.

As the Laugherty family walked along the street, they could smell the sweet aromas of sweets – Turkish delight, peppermint, truffles, liquorice, aniseed, chocolate, minty humbugs, marzipan, cough candy and nougat. Right next to the sweet shop, of course, was the curiosity shop. As the children looked in the window of the sweet shop they noticed a chocolate advent clock named Clementine Advent. The children rushed into the shop and bought the chocolate advent clock, and they rushed out again without even knowing they'd been in the shop. They then rushed straight back in again, and this time their parents followed.

The shop also sold milkshakes: the children had

strawberry milkshakes, and Patrick and Penelope had chocolate milkshakes. Patrick noticed that the children had purchased the advent clock that was in the shop window. He guessed it was the advent clock, even though Mabble Merlin had wrapped it in dark-chocolate-coloured shiny wrapping paper and tied it with a coffee-coloured bow.

Clementine Advent had been to Mabble Merlin's Music and Dance School, and she had passed with flying colours. She was so glad to be purchased that day by the Laugherty children and she was looking forward to life in a large Victorian house in London. She hoped she could create a wonderful, magical Christmas atmosphere, and she planned to sing a lovely magical song. Christmas is a magical time, and she hoped to spread a little magic.

Mabble Merlin liked to spread a little magic too, as did Dr Hoot-Hoot (the owl) and Twilight (the Persian cat) and Lucky (the sometimes-invisible cat).

Clementine Advent Starts to Sing

The one and only Clementine Advent was put on the kitchen wall. She was a Twelve Days of Christmas chocolate clock, and she counted down the twelve days before Christmas.

At the stroke of midnight the chocolate clock started to sing, and I must say she had a very sweet voice – it was as sweet as chocolate.

On the twelfth day before Christmas at midnight all of the Laugherty household was quiet, and a magical feeling of Christmas hung in the air. It was a lovely atmosphere. Then all of a sudden Clementine Advent started to sing:

"On the first day of Christmas
My true love sent to me . . ."

Then instead of singing the words she sang to the music: "De de de, da da, de de, da da da, de de de, da da, la la la la la, ta, ta, ta, ta, ta. . . ."

Milly started to sing along, and then the wristwatch sitting on the kitchen top (Omega Horizon) started to sing along, and the grandfather clock in the hall (George Midnight) sang and swayed to the music in a booming voice: "De de, da da da, de de, da da da. . . ." The Australian Clock (Polly Quazar) sang along in her Australian voice: "De de, da da da, de de, da da da. . . . And the picture clock (London Melody) also started to sing along while showing a lovely scene of London with the Christmas lights and the Christmas tree in Trafalgar Square. And the cuckoo clock (Jasmine Feathersprings) joined in too: "De de, da da da, de de, da da da. . . ." In fact, soon every clock and watch in the house was singing along.

Unexpectedly, the cranberry jelly in the fridge started to sing along as it wibbled and wobbled: "De de, da da da, de de, da da da. . . ." Then Midnight Owl in the oak tree in the garden started to hoot along: "Hoot hoot hoot, de de, da da da. . . ."

Unexpectedly, and strangely enough, the fridge door swung open with a blast of cool air and the dead turkey cock took to his feet. Even though he was without his head, he started to strut his funky stuff on the tiled kitchen floor: "De de, da da da," he sang in his beautiful turkey voice:

"On the first day of Christmas
My true love sent to me
A partridge in a pear tree.
On the second day of Christmas
My true love sent to me
Two turtle doves
And a partridge in a pear tree."

Then the ice cubes in the fridge shook like maraccas and shouted, "That's brrrilliant!" They shivered and quivered and then piped up in shrill tones:

"On the third day of Christmas
My true love sent to me
Three French hens,
Two turtle doves
And a partridge in a pear tree."

Then Mog Og, who had been sleeping soundly, woke up and stepped into the kitchen. He started to caterwaul in his lovely voice, and accompanying himself by using his long whiskers as a fiddle he sang:

"On the fourth day of Christmas
My true love sent to me
Four calling birds,
Three French hens,
Two turtle doves
And a partridge in a pear tree."

He danced round the kitchen, singing with the headless turkey, and then he danced through the cat flap out into the garden where Midnight Owl was singing in the apple tree. He danced under the tree and then he started to run and jump and skip. He was so happy! He ran along the cobbled lanes, still singing, and the alley cats joined in with him, and he ran through hedges, over ditches and bridges singing all the while.

When he came to quilted fields of corn and barley and wheat, the swaying crops began humming along: "De, da da da da. . . ."

And in a farmyard not too far away, under dreaming skies, the silly cows began to sing along with Mog Og:

"On the fifth day of Christmas
My true love sent to me
Five gold rings,
Four calling birds,
Three French hens,
Two turtle doves
And a partridge in a pear tree."

And then the porky pigs in the pigpen started to sing along

with Mog Og: "De, da, de, da da, de de, da da da. . . ." and they snorted as they sang.

And then the geese gaggling in the farmyard started to sing with their lovely gaggling voices:

> "On the sixth day of Christmas
> My true love sent to me
> Six geese a-laying,
> Five gold rings,
> Four calling birds,
> Three French hens,
> Two turtle doves
> And a partridge in a pear tree."

Then the sheep in the fields heard the singing and started to sing along as well. They piped up in their baa-baa voices:

> "On the seventh day of Christmas
> My true love sent to me
> Seven swans a-swimming,
> Six geese a-laying,
> Five gold rings,
> Four calling birds,
> Three French hens,
> Two turtle doves
> And a partridge in a pear tree."

Even some very, very early morning milkmaids milking the cows started to sing in their milkmaid voices:

> "On the eighth day of Christmas
> My true love sent to me
> Eight maids a-milking,
> Seven swans a-swimming,
> Six geese a-laying,

Five gold rings,
Four calling birds,
Three French hens,
Two turtle doves
And a partridge in a pear tree."

Then the early morning milkman struck up a note as he carried his bottles of milk in the quiet, sleepy village. The milkman sang:

"On the ninth day of Christmas
My true love sent to me
Nine ladies dancing,
Eight maids a-milking,
Seven swans a-swimming,
Six geese a-laying,
Five gold rings . . ."

In the manor house on the hill, the lord and lady of the manor suddenly started singing in their sleep:

"On the tenth day of Christmas
My true love sent to me
Ten lords a-leaping,
Nine ladies dancing,
Eight maids a-milking,
Seven swans a-swimming,
Six geese a-laying,
Five gold rings,
Four calling birds,
Three French hens,
Two turtle doves
And a partridge in a pear tree."

There was a castle on another hill, and Mog Og danced

into the courtyard, where he sang while the pipers played:

"On the eleventh day of Christmas
My true love sent to me
Eleven pipers piping,
Ten lords a-leaping,
Nine ladies dancing,
Eight maids a-milking,
Seven swans a-swimming,
Six geese a-laying . . ."

Then in the same courtyard Mog Og noticed some strange drummers. They were ghosts from years gone by, but they looked real enough so Mog Og sang while they played:

"On the twelfth day of Christmas
My true love sent to me
Twelve drummers drumming,
Eleven pipers piping,
Ten lords a-leaping,
Nine ladies dancing,
Eight maids a-milking,
Seven swans a-swimming,
Six geese a-laying,
Five gold rings,
Four calling birds,
Three French hens,
Two turtle doves
And a partridge in a pear tree."

Back at the Laugherty house there was a party atmosphere like never before. The clocks all sang together like an orchestra playing.

Mog Og had been singing for a very long time, but eventually he decided to run back home. He ran over hedges, over bridges, over fields, and even over sheep in the fields, until he finally arrived back home. By this time all the clocks had stopped singing and humming, the headless turkey had stopped strutting his funky stuff, the jelly had stopped singing, the ice cubes had stopped singing – everyone had stopped singing.

The house was quiet, and everyone fell asleep, having enjoyed the midnight festivities.

Dr Laugherty came downstairs very early as usual the next morning, and he wondered why on earth the turkey was out of the fridge, lying on the floor, and the jelly was in a heap and the ice cubes were all over the place.

Dr Laugherty didn't have time to clean and tidy the kitchen, so he called Miles to come and put the turkey back in the fridge and tidy the place a little.

He never dreamt that Clementine Advent was the cause of it all. No one would have guessed. She was now sitting on the kitchen wall, not making a sound. The only thing different about her was the fact that a chocolate had been eaten. Daisy had eaten the first advent chocolate on the twelfth day of Christmas.

The Pantomime

In their luxurious living room the real-fir Christmas tree had been put up by Miles. It was very large, with huge sparkling baubles and tinsel and gold and silver bows, and right at the top was Pumby Ely Fuddles, the Christmas fairy whom Penelope had purchased from the Musty Old Magical Curiosity Shop.

The Christmas socks had been hung up beside the log fire in the Victorian living room, which looked very Christmassy. Dr Laugherty had hung his very own socks (washed, of course) from the Victorian mantelpiece, and inside each sock he'd put nuts, apples, oranges and chocolates and a £2 coin. Mog Og could vouch for the fact that the socks were clean. He would often lie on the fluffy fur rug in front of the fire, and he would have known if there were any smelly socks nearby.

The room looked lovely – so pretty and delightful with red, gold, silver, purple and green tinsel, and Christmas cards hung across the wall alcoves. There was mistletoe on the picture clock, London Melody. Everything was festive, and they were all as high as kites with the excitement and the festive mood.

The Laugherty family planned to go to the Christmas Eve pantomime at a theatre in Drury Lane, about fifteen minutes from where they lived.

Dr Laugherty had decided to get into the festive spirit by hiring a 'Santa sleigh'.

Little did he know that it came originally from the Musty Old Magical Curiosity Shop, and the sleigh and the reindeer were able to fly magically through the air.

The Laugherty family excitedly grabbed their hats, coats, scarves and gloves. It was a cold night and it looked like it could snow. They all climbed on to the 'Santa sleigh' and set off for the Petticoat Theatre in Drury Lane to watch the pantomime, which was called *The Musty Old Magical Curiosity Shop*.

When they arrived at the theatre they took their seats in the front row. The children noticed some of their friends from school, who were sitting a few seats along on the same row. These friends were Sophia Louise and Laura Lou and Craig Anthony, and they were with their parents, Mr and Mrs Lemonade.

The Laugherty family had a box of popcorn, and the Lemonade family were eating hot dogs and drinking lemonade.

Daisy and Oliver suddenly wanted some lemonade, so Patrick went to the theatre shop and got four cartons of lemonade. He thought it was a bit silly the Lemonade family drinking lemonade – he hoped he didn't start laughing. Then he remembered he had an unusual name, and some people might think the Laugherty family laughed all of the time. Some neighbours of his were named Mr and Mrs Rice, and he wondered if they cooked rice all the time, or if they loved rice.

Eventually he got back to his seat – and the seats were very plush crimson velvet, matching the heavy crimson velvet curtains which hung across the stage. As they watched, the curtains slowly opened, revealing a large sign which read, 'The Musty Old Magical Curiosity Shop'. It shone iridescent in the purple light. It looked amazing.

The pantomime was in fact based on a true story; and it was indeed a funny story and an amazing one, but the story had actually happened.

The audience watched in awe as large buildings appeared in front of them. In the first scene they saw the Sands of Time Hotel with its revolving glass doors and a large iridescent Sands of Time egg timer in the hallway. The hotel was situated in the Bayswater area, and there was a zebra crossing at the corner of the street. There wasn't heavy traffic, but there was a steady flow.

Two American tourists were standing outside the hotel – Cynthia and Tobias Chimes. They had decided to go to Stonehenge, which was a place they had always wanted to go to, and they were waiting for a taxi to take them there. They looked left and then right to see if the taxi was on its way; and then Cynthia looked left again and noticed a shop. It was not just any shop, but the Musty Old Magical Curiosity Shop. They both rushed back into the hotel through the revolving doors, where the hotel owner, Claude Monet, a Frenchman dressed in a beret and typical French clothes, was concentrating on painting a picture on his easel. The painting looked extremely brilliant, just like a famous artist's painting, and, strangely enough, it was of the street outside. Claude was splashing on the colour, using a palette with every colour you can imagine on it. In the painting the audience could clearly see the front of the hotel and the Musty Old Magical Curiosity Shop beside it.

Tobias asked Claude Monet if he'd ever seen the shop before. He didn't say he had seen it, and he didn't say he hadn't seen it; he said he'd seen a lot of strange things – even upside-down rain – in London. He told them they should take a look inside the Musty Old Magical Curiosity Shop instead of going to Stonehenge, as they could go to Stonehenge on another day. He said he was sure Stonehenge wasn't about to disappear – he knew it was a very magical place, but he had never heard of it disappearing.

The Laugherty family ate their popcorn and drank their lemonade, shuffled in their seats and became engrossed in the pantomime. It actually seemed as if it was actually happening, or as if it had actually happened.

On the stage the two American tourists had rushed into the Musty Old Magical Curiosity Shop.

Daisy and Oliver felt sure they had seen the shop somewhere before, and Patrick and Penelope also felt they'd seen it somewhere before.

The shopkeeper, whose name was Mabble Merlin, was dressed in a Victorian suit – the kind of suit that was fashionable in the 1860s.

The Laugherty family couldn't take their eyes off the stage. They were mesmerised. The shop was full to the brim with all sorts of things, including what looked like antiques from hundreds of years ago and things that looked as though they came from thousands of years ago, and things that looked as though they came from the age of the dinosaur. There were things from every century and every planet and they all looked as good as new, without scratches. Nothing was in need of repair. Everything was old, but looked as though it had just been made.

Suddenly Daisy and Oliver got a shock. They noticed a cat in the shop window, and it looked almost exactly like Mog Og. The only thing different was that its fur kept changing colour, from grey to black to stripy, to tortoiseshell, to ginger, to white, to black-and-white, to brown. Luckily it didn't change to blue or pink or red or orange or purple, and it didn't change to green. When it finally changed back to grey, it looked exactly like Mog Og.

Unknown to the Laugherty family, it actually was Mog Og.

The Lemonade family laughed so much at the cat changing colour that they nearly fell off their seats. If they had known it was Mog Og, the Laugherty family's silly cat, they would definitely have fallen off their seats.

Mog Og couldn't think what on earth he was doing in the shop window of the Musty Old Magical Curiosity Shop. When he looked out through the window of the shop, he could see all the people in their seats in the theatre. He felt weird! He thought he was probably dreaming.

He looked up and saw an owl in a tree, so he decided to ask the owl in the tree. He had a feeling he'd seen the owl before, and it came into his head that the owl would know anything he asked.

"Have you any idea what I'm doing in this shop window?" he asked.

"You're in a Christmas pantomime, Mog Og. You're a hero, and now you're a star too, and everyone's come to the pantomime to see you. You're a magical cat, and that's why your fur keeps changing colour."

"Well, surely it's just a dream, isn't it, Mr Owl? I was just at home in front of the log fire. I was on the fluffy rug dreaming – or actually, I think I was talking to someone, but I can't recall who."

"It was the magical fairy, Pumby Ely Fuddles, who was sitting on the top of the Christmas tree. She used her magical powers to magic you here along with all of the clocks."

"Along with all of the clocks! You mean George Midnight, the grandfather clock; and Milly Paris, the French clock; and London Melody, the picture clock; and Jasmine Feathersprings; and the Australian clock, Polly Quazar?"

"Yes, and even Omega Horizon and the other wristwatches, if they were doing nothing. Pumby Ely Fuddles wanted to use her magical powers to magic all of you here to make you all stars. She wanted you to see your name in lights – and now you all have! It's a wish come true.

Now Cynthia and Tobias were in the shop and Mabble Merlin was offering to take them on the trip of a lifetime.

Mabble Merlin pressed a button, and the Laugherty family saw the shop till disappear and a control panel popped up. They saw Cynthia and Tobias sitting in reclining seats and they heard Mabble Merlin asking them where they wanted to go. Tobias decided to go to the year 1533, and the audience saw the Musty Old Magical Curiosity Shop lift into the air and whizz off into the night sky, making a strange beeping and gurgling sound as it went.

Everyone in the audience went, "Wow!"

The shop zoomed through outer space and then the stars of the cosmos appeared as the shop floated through deep space. Then the 'spacers', Xanadu and Galaxy, appeared on a plasma screen above the control panel and offered refreshments to Cynthia and Tobias and Captain Mabble Merlin.

After the shop had gone through deep space and through a wormhole it eventually arrived in Tudor times in the year 1533. When the lights came up on the stage, the audience saw the amazing accommodation above the shop, and the next scene showed the wedding of King Henry VIII and Anne Boleyn. The audience watched, mesmerised, and they were very sad when Anne Boleyn had to be cloned because King Henry wanted to chop her head off.

The funniest scene was the pie fight with the Four Just Men. One of the pies hit someone in the audience, but the audience all clapped and thought it was hilarious. They thought the wedding was funny too – how they danced to the Beatles music and other funky tunes – and the audience wondered if anyone would notice Tobias taking photographs all the time.

The Travellers Return

Although Cynthia and Tobias felt as though they were in Tudor times for a few years (from 1533 until 1536), when the Musty Old Magical Curiosity Shop came back it had really only been gone for a few hours, or so it seemed! For Mog Og and the clocks it seemed like an even shorter time than that.

The Musty Old Magical Curiosity Shop beamed itself back to the year 2010, bringing with it Cynthia and Tobias, the twelve musicians and the real Anne Boleyn.

Cynthia and Tobias were glad to be back. In a little way they had really enjoyed Tudor times, but they wouldn't have liked to live without running water and power showers and toilets and plasma televisions and telephones and all life's other luxuries, like duvets and feather pillows. It was OK for the trip of a lifetime, but they were glad to be back.

All of a sudden, in the Petticoat Theatre, all of the clocks and Mog Og started to sing:

> "On the twelfth day of Christmas
> My true love sent to me . . ."

The twelve musicians from King Henry's court started to sing along and play their musical instruments, and Anne Boleyn started to sing along too. Cynthia and Tobias joined in:

"On the first day of Christmas
My true love sent to me
A partridge in a pear tree."

And the twelve musicians sang:

"On the second day of Christmas
My true love sent to me
Two turtle doves
And a partridge in a pear tree."

And Mog Og sang along, and all the clocks joined in, and
the Laugherty family hummed along to the song, and so did
the Lemonade family, and all the audience joined in. They
thought it was an excellent evening – and an amazing
pantomime! They didn't know which part they loved the
most.

The Butler Knows Something

Miles went into the living room and then the dining room and then the kitchen and hallway to make sure the house was clean and tidy for Christmas Day. Before the family returned from the pantomime, strangely enough, he realised Mog Og was missing from the fluffy rug where he had been sleeping five minutes before.

He then discovered that George Midnight was missing, and soon after that he found that all the clocks were missing.

Suddenly Pumby Ely Fuddles, the Christmas fairy, appeared in the middle of the room. She looked very pretty, with her long, dark hair tumbling down her back and her pretty pink dress with feathers at the hem and her pretty silvery-pink wings and sky-blue eyes. Pumby waved her silver wand and sprinkled fairy dust over Miles.

Miles wanted to tell the fairy that the clocks and Mog Og were missing. He tried to speak, but she whispered, "I'm Pumby Ely Fuddles, a magical fairy with magical powers. Don't worry, Miles. They'll be back by midnight. You've been a very, very busy butler. Have a rest; put your feet up; lay your weary self in the leather armchair. The dusting has been done; the crockery is washed." (Miles always rushed around, trying to get things prepared.)

Just before midnight all the clocks and Mog Og came back, as if by magic. Mog Og had really enjoyed being in the pantomime, and so had all the clocks.

The Laugherty family really enjoyed the pantomime. Daisy and Oliver enjoyed the pie fight the most, but Patrick and Penelope enjoyed the wedding the best.

Cynthia and Tobias enjoyed everything. They came out of the shop and went into the hotel next door – the Sands of Time Hotel. When they asked to book a room, Claude Monet said one had already been booked for them and their bags were in storage and their bill had been paid.

When the Laugherty family got back from the pantomime the clocks were all in their places, exactly as they left them. Well, not quite all: George Midnight had been a bit dented and he was a little to the left of where he normally stood, and London Melody was crooked. The other clocks had been crooked as well, but Miles had straightened them up before the Laugherty family came in.

When Miles woke up after his rest, he thought he'd had a lovely dream about the fairy on the Christmas tree.

Mog Og was glad to be back on the rug in front of the fire, and he was glad his fur wasn't changing colour any more.

The Laugherty family told Miles they really enjoyed the pantomime, and they said it looked as though Mog Og and all the clocks were on stage, but Miles decided not to say much about his experience. He just told the Laugherty family that he had had a little glass of sherry and sat down for five minutes in the armchair and had a strange dream that the clocks and Mog Og went missing. He said he woke up startled as he thought it was real, but, when he went to check, everything was in its place, but just a little bit crooked.

"I was so relieved that it was just a dream," said Miles to the Laugherty family.

The Laugherty family had thought the pantomime was spectacular, and they thought they would have an extra-special Christmas.